Death Rattle

Death Rattle

Jory Sherman

THORNDIKE PRESS
A part of Gale, Cengage Learning

GALE
CENGAGE Learning™

Detroit • New York • San Francisco • New Haven, Conn • Waterville, Maine • London

Thorndike Press® Large Print Western.
The text of this Large Print edition is unabridged.
Other aspects of the book may vary from the original edition.
Set in 16 pt. Plantin.

LIBRARY OF CONGRESS CATALOGING-IN-PUBLICATION DATA

Sherman, Jory.
Death rattle / by Jory Sherman.
p. cm. — (Thorndike Press large print Western)
ISBN-13: 978-1-4104-3786-0 (hardcover)
ISBN-10: 1-4104-3786-8 (hardcover)
1. Large type books. I. Title.
PS3569.H43D43 2011
813'.54—dc22 2011008969

Published in 2011 by arrangement with The Berkley Publishing Group, a member of Penguin Group (USA), Inc.

Printed in the United States of America
1 2 3 4 5 6 7 15 14 13 12 11

For Stephen Woodfin

One

The stagecoach lurched and swayed as it rounded a bend in the rough mountain road. The driver, Quincy "Quince" Mepps, braced himself for the turn. "Lean to the right, Hugh," he said to the young man riding shotgun. Quince leaned against Hugh as the stage rounded the turn. Hugh Pendergast set the shotgun in his left hand down at his feet and braced himself with his right hand. He felt the tug of gravity, but the wheels stayed down. He heard the creak of metal and wood and leather as the coach careened around the rocky outcropping. Dust spooled behind the stage in twin funnels that merged into a rose-tinted tawny cloud.

The rocky road descended into a saddle cavity, then rose in a steep incline. The four-horse team strained against their traces as they began the climb. The coach slowed and both men leaned forward as if to defy the gravity that pulled at them and the coach.

"Giddyap," shouted Quince as he cracked the reins against the rumps of the hind horses. "Always hated this hill," he told Hugh. "A bitch-willy, for sure."

"I don't like it," Hugh said.

"That intuition of your'n again, Hugh?"

"More like a gut instinct, Quince."

"Hell, they's better places for bandits than this blamed hill." He grunted against the slow tug of the weight beneath them that slowed the coach.

"It's all them rocks up at the top, Quince. They bother me ever' time we struggle up this grade."

"Mountains is all rocks," Quince said.

"Those are ambush rocks."

Quince snorted, looked at Hugh with a merry-cheeked grin as the coach slowed even more and the horses struggled to pull the load, four chests billowing out as they breathed, veins streaking to the surface of their legs.

"Come on, boys," Quince urged the team, "bust on up to the top."

The horses cleared the top of the incline, and the coach lumbered up behind them and stopped dead as a large rock rolled in front of the right rear wheel. Then another rock rolled in front of the left front wheel.

The spokes groaned and one of them cracked with a sound like that of a bone breaking.

One of the lead horses whinnied and shied away from a man-sized shape that emerged from the jumble of rocks.

The coach stopped dead in its tracks as the other horses dug in their hooves and backed away from the threat. Another man jumped in front of the lead horse on the left flank. He grabbed the reins with both hands and pulled the horse's head down. The horse's neck bowed, and it snorted steam and snot through its nostrils.

Quince grabbed the brake handle and pulled it back. This was an instinctive action as he felt his stomach wrench at the sudden stop. He tried to stand up to see what had stopped the team, but a man stepped up on the coach and laid a sawed-off shotgun hard against Quince's belly.

"You just sit tight," the man said. "Drop them reins."

Quince opened his hands and the reins fell out of them like dead snakes.

Hugh reached for the shotgun at his feet.

He heard two loud clicks from the man who had Quince braced against the back of the seat.

"You just sit tight, sonny," the man with

the shotgun said.

"We ain't got no strongbox," Quince said, as if that information would make the man go away and leave them be.

"Shut up," Shotgun said.

Two more men came out from behind the rocks. Both were on horseback. They, like the others, wore yellow hoods over their faces. The hoods looked like bleached flour sacks dipped in yellow dye.

One of the men on horseback rode up and stuck a rifle in Quince's face. He cocked it, and Shotgun jumped down, no longer needed.

The second horseman rode up to Hugh and drew his pistol, a Colt .45 with bone grips that were etched brown with deep grooves.

"You Hugh Pendergast? Harry's son?" the man said. He cocked the Colt's hammer back and the click made Hugh jerk as though electrocuted.

"Y-yes," Hugh stammered.

"That's all I wanted to know," the man said. He shoved the barrel flush against Hugh's forehead and pulled the trigger.

The back of Hugh's head exploded into a cloud of crimson spray, and pieces of shattered bone flew back. A black hole appeared in Hugh's forehead. His head snapped back, and then all the life went out of his neck. He slumped over, his mouth open in a silent scream, his eyes glossed over with the final frost of death: vacant, sightless.

Smoke curled out of the shooter's pistol barrel, made a lazy spiral as the man swung the snout over to fix on Quince.

"You tell Harry Pendergast to get off my tail, Quince. This is just a warning."

Quince's eyes narrowed to slits.

He recognized the voice, and he felt the clammy clutch of fear deep in his belly.

"The silver's in the boot," Quince said, his voice quavering with fear. He sounded as if he was shivering in a cold wind.

"I know where it is," the man said. He nodded to Shotgun and the other man on horseback, who rode around to the back of the coach. Shotgun opened the boot and began removing silver bars. He handed them up to the man on horseback, who filled two gunnysacks, tied them together, and slung them over his pommel.

"You sit here for ten minutes, Quince, then drive your team on into Denver. You be sure to tell Harry what I said, hear?"

"Yeah, I hear you," Quince said. A series of tremors ran through his upraised hands. His mouth was dry, his lips bloodless.

The man holstered his pistol and wheeled

his horse. The other men walked back behind the rocks. Quince heard the creak of leather as they mounted their horses. A few seconds later, he heard the scrape of iron hooves on stone, the crunch of gravel, then the pounding gallop of at least a half dozen horses. He lowered his hands, bent down, and picked up the slack ends of his reins. He sat there until he no longer heard the hoofbeats, sat there with his eyes fixed on the body of Hugh Pendergast, Harry's son.

Pendergast's Denver Detective Agency was now short one man, and the Panamint Mining Company was out some five thousand dollar's worth of silver bullion. And maybe, he thought, the Leadville Stage would soon be short a driver.

The man who had killed Hugh was Earl Fincher. Quince was pretty damned sure of that.

And Earl Fincher was a man to be feared, like no other.

Two

The three riders rode up to the outcroppings on both sides of the road.

A hawk sailed ahead of them on invisible currents of air, dragging its rumpled shadow over the wagon ruts. It disappeared over the rim of the road.

Brad Storm examined the wagon ruts. They were deeper where the stage had stopped. He saw boot tracks in the dust and, alongside, the shoe prints of a horse.

"This is where they jumped us," Quince said. "We come to a dead stop and before I knew what was happenin', one of 'em came up from behind those rocks and shoved a sawed-off Greener in my face. Two of 'em held the lead horses, so we was stuck."

"Is this where . . ." Harry Pendergast stammered.

"Yes, sir, Mr. Pendergast. Another'n rode up from the left side and asked —"

"Asked what?" Pendergast said.

"Asked Hugh if he was your son."

Harry Pendergast cringed, and his face drained of color. Sweat oozed from under his hat and crawled down his forehead like rainwater. Tears filled Pendergast's eyes, and he squinched them shut as if to block out Quince's words.

Brad turned his horse and rode over to the two men.

"It's just like you said, Quince," he said. "Two men came around to the boot. I guess they knew the silver bars were in there."

"Yeah, they did."

"You know who those two men were?" Brad asked.

"Nope, just the one what shot Hugh. I recognized his voice."

"Earl Fincher," Pendergast said.

Streaks of clouds hovered in the western sky, white and purple against the blue. The sun was a piercing light that shimmered above the snowcapped peaks of the mountain range, a boiling disk of yellow fire.

Brad looked at Harry without comprehension. The name meant nothing to Storm. Harry's wet eyes seemed to swim in sadness from their sockets. He looked out of place on the sorrel horse he rode, with his business suit, brocade vest, riding boots, starched white shirt, and bolo tie, the pert black derby on his head. They had all met at the Oro City Livery early that morning. Quince had ridden up to Brad's ranch the night before with the sad news and the message from Pendergast that his son had been murdered. Quince had told him the whole story about the holdup, saying five men had jumped him and Hugh a week ago. There had been no rain and the tracks of the stagecoach and the horses and bandits had not been erased by wind or water.

The sorrel horse Pendergast rode looked as uncomfortable as Harry. It rolled its baleful eyes at Ginger, Brad's roan gelding, as if beseeching Ginger to get him out from under Pendergast.

"Never heard of him," Brad said.

Quince looked off at the sky, staring at a single wisp of cloud as if he wished he were miles away from this place of death.

"I caused the arrest of Fincher about six years ago," Pendergast said. "He did three years in Cañon City for robbery."

"So?" Brad said.

"I suspected him of murder but couldn't prove it."

"You think that's why he murdered your son?" Brad said.

Harry's eyes narrowed in a scowl, and he looked off at the side of the road where grasses grew in desperate clumps among the small rocks and the little islands of prickly pear cactus. He stared at the bleak landscape far off the road, and it all blurred together in a meaningless jumble of empty land devoid of life.

"I've sent for Pete Farnsworth," Pendergast said. "He should be in Leadville by tonight. You'll meet him at the Clarendon."

"What's that have to do with Earl Fincher?" Brad asked.

Harry heaved a sigh and looked at Quince.

"Some months ago, I was contacted by a man, I won't tell you his name, who told me he and other mine and smelter owners were being held up by a gang of hard cases. These hard cases wore yellow hoods and demanded what they called 'protection money.' At first, none of those owners acceded to these requests. Then the robberies and the beatings began. This man hired my agency to find these men and put them out of business."

Brad felt the weight of what Pendergast was telling him. Hooded men with guns. Faceless men. Brutal men. Killers.

"I don't think it's just the mine and smelter owners these men are holding up," Brad said.

"What do you mean?" Pendergast asked.

"My wife, Felicity, said the prices of food and goods had gone up in town, and when she asked why, nobody would tell her. Then I sold some cattle at auction a week ago, and had to pay a higher percentage of the sale. When I asked why, the man told me he was paying higher cartage fees and more for feed. But he wouldn't tell me more than that, and when I asked, he looked scared and made damned sure nobody but me could hear him. So maybe this gang is widening its loop."

"I spoke to the sheriff in Leadville," Harry said, "and he told me he didn't know anything about a gang wearing yellow hoods."

"Did you believe him?" Brad asked.

"At the time, yes. I think you and Pete might ask again. If they're holding up people in town, the sheriff has to know about it. Sheriff I asked was named Rodney Dimsdale, and he was elected after the previous sheriff was killed mysteriously."

"What do you mean 'mysteriously'?"

"He supposedly fell off his horse and broke his neck. But witnesses Pete talked to said Sheriff Brown was brutally beaten at his home."

"Lou Brown," Brad said. "I wondered about that. Word was that he was breaking a horse and it threw him."

"I think differently," Pendergast said.

"All this talk gives me the willies," Quince said. "I knowed Lou, and I met Rodney Dimsdale. Voted for him."

"Lou was a straight arrow," Brad said, "and he knew horses. I bought one from him, one he broke himself. It was tame as a tabby cat.

"But you said Dimsdale was the new sheriff?"

"Well, Dimsdale was shot and killed, so that's more for you and Pete to look into, Brad. Will you meet with him at the Clarendon tonight?"

"Or tomorrow morning," Brad said. "I'll tell Felicity I'll be away for a time."

"Good," Harry said and reached into his coat pocket. He pulled out a small badge with the legend Denver Detective Agency engraved on its gold and silver surface. "You might need this, Brad." The badge glinted in the sun.

Brad shook his head.

"I won't need it, Harry," he said. "I've got this."

Brad pulled out the thong around his neck and lifted a set of rattles out of his shirt. He shook the thong, and it rattled. Pendergast leaned back in his saddle. Quince's horse whinnied and sidestepped away from the sound.

Harry pulled the badge back, but did not put it in his pocket.

"Maybe you don't need this, after all," he said.

Brad shook the rattle again.

"This is the only badge I need," he said, and let it fall back under his shirt.

"So that's why they call you Sidewinder," Quince said, his voice a breathy whisper. "I wondered."

"And he's just as deadly," Pendergast said.

"I'm going to follow the tracks of those killers, Harry. Maybe I'll learn something about this gang."

"There's a room ready for you at the Clarendon, Brad."

Brad rode past the rocks and waved to Harry and Quince. In moments, he was following the hoofprints well off the road.

There were six men, he determined, not five. And the tracks were heading into rough country, deep in the foothills.

The sky was a pastel blue and the clouds were thickening off to the west as if the mountains were giving birth to white thunderheads that would float down over the plain and darken the land with shadows.

A lone quail piped a warning somewhere

ahead of him, and the silence grew up around him as he followed the tracks of six horses and six men who wore yellow hoods.

THREE

Brad studied the tracks and felt the hackles rise and bristle on the back of his neck. He surveyed the country ahead and around him with an uneasy feeling, a feeling that he was riding into someone else's territory, a forbidden realm where a stranger's life was on the line.

What had he gotten himself into with Pendergast? He had helped the man break up a gang of cattle rustlers, then accepted the dubious job of detective in Pendergast's agency. Harry had assured him that he would be called to duty only when absolutely necessary but would receive a monthly retainer just to be on call. And Brad had needed the money, both to restock his decimated herd of cattle and to build his ranch some miles into the mountains above Leadville.

And now this.

This tug of Fate once again. A tug that

was pulling him away from Felicity and his ranch, away from the peace and tranquillity of his own land in the mountains, into the night-marish crush of civilization with its men of greed and lust, its corruption of the flesh, its disease-bearing malignancy of a man's soul.

He patted his hand on the bedroll tied behind his saddle, the full saddlebags. Felicity had done that, with Julio Aragon's help, of course. She made sure he had bedding and food when he had told her he was just riding down into town with Quince to see Pendergast. He had told her, "I'll be back home by sundown."

"Just in case," she had said. Then she had embraced him, kissed him long and lingeringly before he mounted Ginger and rode off shortly after dawn, a dawn that cracked the eyes with its blaze of peach and salmon colors, its scent of sage and fir and pine, its gray mist rising off the land, off the dew-flocked backs of his cattle, and Julio waving goodbye with a wide grin cracking his sun-bronzed face.

Both of them had packed his supplies, he thought, as if they knew he would not be back home this day, and maybe not the next.

What in hell was he doing? he asked himself as he followed the single line of tracks, knowing that the outlaws were following the same path back to the place from whence they had come. Two sets of horse tracks, going and coming. Plain to read, and chilling to behold. Six men, all armed, all wearing yellow hoods because they did not want to be identified. Cowardly men, hiding their faces under masks.

He didn't know this part of the country. He was south of Leadville, he knew, and he could almost smell the prairie that lay beyond the rugged foothills and the mountains. The land was broken with ravines, gullies, and low ridges that hid what lay past them. He could not see more than an eighth of a mile beyond the line of horse tracks. A dangerous place to be, yet his hunch was that the tracks would lead to Leadville, or someplace near there. From the looks of the tracks, those men he pursued were long gone. Already, the edges of the tracks were crumbling, turning to dust.

This was a game trail, he decided, not heavily traveled, although he saw signs of deer, rabbit, and quail droppings. Nothing fresh. The trail wound through brush and down a shallow ravine, then topped a small ridge before leading down the other side to a stretch of flat land. He kept looking around him, above and below the trail to see if anyone might be watching. He had the feeling that he was alone and that nobody was expecting him to follow this path to wherever it led.

He kept expecting the tracks to lead back up to the stage road, but they didn't. Instead, they followed a southeasterly course into even more desolate and deserted country. Finally, the game trail petered out, and the tracks became harder to follow. The land grew more rugged, with low mounds dotted with prickly pear and sage, spiky Spanish bayonets, and cholla. The tracks were no longer in a straight line, but were separated, as if the outlaws had ridden in formation, six men on horseback, four or five feet apart, as if they were nearing their destination.

The tracks led Brad to a rocky hardpan on a wide plain. To his surprise, the riders had fallen into single file once again, and, as he soon learned, they were riding in a straight line along the same path they had taken. The trail was a moil of tracks going in both directions, yet he was certain none of the riders had taken such a path before the day they rode off to kill Hugh Pendergast.

"Pretty smart," he muttered to himself. At least one of the men was likely a tracker himself. And, Brad surmised, at least one of them must have scouted the terrain before any of them set out to stop the stage from Leadville. Yet, as he surveyed the terrain, he could not see any other tracks on either side of the narrow trail. There was no broken ground, no overturned rocks, no damaged brush.

The days-old tracks were fading fast on the hardpan, the edges wafted into dust by the winds, the strong breezes that blew across the small plateau. At least one man had known that that was likely to happen and had led the others across this stretch. The plateau began to narrow and grow smaller. Brad strained his eyes to make out the maze of tracks. By the time he got to the end, they were all but invisible, the ground scoured by strong breezes and violent winds. As soon as he reached the edge, a strong gust of wind struck him in the face and he felt grains of sand sting his cheeks. He bowed his head and pulled the brim of his hat lower over his face.

The wind blew from a deep ravine off to his right, so narrow it was like a roofless funnel. The hardpan vanished and he rode through thick brush and heavy sand, downward into a grassy stretch that was almost like prairie. Clumps of prickly pear and stalks of yucca fought for dominion among small stunted pines that had taken hold along a narrow stretch of land where the winds from the plains met the zephyrs streaming down from the mountains. He felt the stings of dust flung from the west, and he narrowed his eyes as he struggled to make out the faint spoor of six horses in single file.

Finally, the tracks faded in the maze of cactus, sage, and stunted pines, the spikes of Spanish bayonets and clumps of gama grass.

Brad felt as if he had descended into a desolate hell where even the wildlife feared to tread. And, as he gazed ahead of him, he saw only more jumbled land that looked as though something with giant claws had once roamed through this empty lowland and torn up the ground with its gigantic talons. Here, there were no landmarks, no definition of terrain that his senses might grasp and understand.

Here, there was only desolation and trackless earth where the winds swirled and danced like dervishes. He saw a small dust devil form several yards away, and Ginger shied at the swirl of dust that seemed to grow in size as it moved across their path and headed for the distant, unseen plain.

He turned Ginger toward higher ground, tapping his flanks with his spurs. He could no longer see the snowcapped peaks to the west and felt as if he were in some kind of huge bowl that could swallow all who passed through its center. Ginger climbed up a steep incline toward a ridge that promised to give Brad a better view of the land ahead.

When he reached the ridgeline, both he and Ginger were winded, and he reined the horse to a stop.

There was no sign of life as far as he could see, and a stiff wind made his shirt flap and rattled the brim of his hat.

Then he saw it, far off, just barely above the horizon. He almost missed it, but there it was, floating just above the farthest point of land to the south, a faint scrim of black smoke, a serpentine scrawl that swirled and snaked into the sky, then vanished like some desert mirage.

He looked off to the bulging clouds boiling over the foothills, blotting out the mountains. They darkened as he watched, and he saw the tracings of summer lightning flicker in their depths, soundless and far away, but brilliant as polished silver.

He shivered as his spine tingled with a sudden gust of chilled wind.

FOUR

Earl Fincher stood outside the building, a ladle full of water held to his lips. He watched the two riders approaching from the west, then dropped the ladle back in the well bucket. He stepped to one side, cupped the beard stubble that flocked his chin, then turned to call out to one of his men who stood in the doorway.

"I only see two riders, Abe."

Abe Danner stepped from the doorway to the hard ground. He peered at the two riders.

"Yep, Finch, ain't but Lenny and Giles a-comin'."

"Where in hell is Cole?"

Abe walked over to the well to stand beside Fincher, who was a head taller and several pounds thinner than the squat form of the pudgy-bellied Danner.

"Hell, I don't know, Finch. Maybe Cole got drunk at the Clarendon and they left him there."

"If he did, it'll be his last drink," Fincher said, a mirthless smile on his hatchet-thin face. "He knows the rules."

"Yeah, he does. I was just makin' a joke, Finch. Cole's a good man. A little loco, maybe, but a good man."

"We'll see what Lenny has to say."

Fincher fished a cheroot from his shirt pocket, stuck it in his mouth. He did not light it as he and Danner waited for the two riders.

When Lenny Carmichael and Giles Becker rode up, they both took off their hats and wiped sweat from their foreheads. Carmichael looked at the smokestack spewing black fumes into the sky from one of the buildings in the old abandoned smelter that served as headquarters for Fincher and his men. There were played-out mines surrounding the smelter, some with considerable tailings, and there was a slag heap several yards away from the building where the smoke was rising from a stone chimney. Both men were wearing sheep-skin-lined jackets. Both were covered with a thin patina of dun-colored dust.

"Storm's a-comin', Finch," Carmichael said. "It's colder'n a bitch up in Leadville."

"Where in hell is Cole?"

"A lot I got to tell you, boss," Carmichael said.

"It had better be good, Lenny."

"Soon as we put up the horses and you pour me some good whiskey, Finch."

"Get to it, both of you," Fincher said. He turned to Abe. "Let's go inside, break out the whiskey. There's a hell of a storm a-comin'."

"I seen the lightning and them black clouds," Abe said, jerking a jaunty thumb at the western horizon.

"Can't hear the thunder yet, so it's still far off."

The two men turned to the clapboard building with its coal black sides.

"Gonna be a gully washer for sure, Finch."

A gust of wind caught the two men as they reached the door, stung the backs of their necks with grit. Jagged streaks of lightning laced the distant black clouds with quicksilver in a soundless display of pyrotechnics along a wide front.

The two men pushed through the doorway. Abe pushed the door shut against the brunt of the wind that gusted in their wake. He rubbed sand from the back of his neck and shivered from the cold chill that gripped him.

Fincher walked through a darkened room

toward a glow of yellow lamplight in another part of the compound. He opened the door and doffed his hat. Abe's wife, Holly, looked up from her sewing at a small table in one corner. She had pieces of yellow cloth stacked at one side and another piece in her hand, cut to resemble the shape of a bell. She finished a stitch and tied off the thread, cutting it with her teeth.

"They got the silver melted and poured, Finch," she said. "I like the heat comin' through the door. It was getting chilly in here."

Abe entered the room and looked at his wife as he lifted his hat from his head. He put it on a wooden peg in the wall. Holly smiled at him, her blue eyes twinkling in the lamplight. She was as pudgy as Abe with streaks of gray twining through her dark hair, which was tied tightly in a bun with a scrap of yellow felt.

Fincher tossed his hat to Abe, who hung it on another wooden peg set in a one-by-four board nailed to the wall.

"I'll tell 'em to keep the furnace burnin'," he said to Holly.

"Is it going to rain?" she asked.

Abe answered her. "Like a cow pissin' on a flat rock," he said.

"Abey!" she said.

Abe walked over to a wooden tool chest and opened the lid. He reached down, and bottles clanked with a sound like Saturday night at the Leadville Saloon. He lifted up a bottle of Old Taylor and carried it to another table in the center of the room, a long scarred slab of cedar sitting on four half stumps that had been debarked and polished to a high sheen. He sat down and opened the bottle.

"Finch, they's glasses in that cabinet above the sink."

"I know where they are," Fincher said and opened the cabinet doors, both of them, as if he were about to do a magic trick. He brought four tumblers over to the table and sat down. He left the cabinet doors open, and the glasses and cups glistened dully in the lamplight. His chair legs scraped over the uneven flooring.

The room was boxlike and bore little resemblance to its former usage as a kind of office and assay room. The sink, of chipped and stained porcelain, had a rusted pipe leading straight down to the floor. The pipe ran outside for several yards but was eaten away in places by rust and was no longer fully buried in the ground.

"Who else is coming?" Holly asked as she pinched the cloth and cut out an eyehole.

"Giles and Lenny," Abe said. He poured whiskey into the tumblers.

"They back from Leadville? What about Cole?" Holly said, pinching the cloth once again to cut the second eyehole.

"Cole didn't come back," Fincher said, looking straight at Holly with her faded gingham dress hiked up above her knees, her bare legs bone white in the dark under the table. He squinched his eyes and thought of his dead wife, Clarabelle, taken by the cholera in '69. But he did not think of her withered body, swollen with their unborn son, or her parched lips, but her soft young face in the rain, her mouth pursed like the folded petals of a flower, her hair wet and curly, her eyes dazzling blue under her long lashes. He felt a twinge course through his gut and turned his head to stare with dull dead eyes at Abe as the man pushed a half-full tumbler toward him.

"To the comin' storm," Abe said.

"Shut up," Fincher said and raised his head slightly as if he were listening for thunder, or something in his imagination, slinking toward him with a scythe in its hands, its skeletal face cowled under a black robe.

"Sure, boss," Abe said, an amiable smile on his lips.

The door opened a few moments later. Carmichael and Becker tramped in, their jackets open, their faces flushed. The wind followed them in and made the lamplight waver until Becker closed the door.

"Whew," Carmichael said. "She's goin' to be a bitch-willy in a hour or two."

The two men hung their hats on pegs and slipped out of their jackets. They hung them on the back of chairs and sat down with a scrape of boots and chair legs.

Fincher glared at Carmichael.

Carmichael pulled a tumbler across the table, reached for the bottle of whiskey.

Fincher grabbed the neck of the bottle and jerked it away from Carmichael.

"First, you tell me about Cole," Fincher said.

"Can't a man even wet his whistle first?"

"No. I want to know why Cole didn't come back with you, Lenny."

Becker licked his lips, stared at the bottle just out of his reach.

Carmichael swallowed hard. He was a lean man with a sharp Adam's apple just under the skin looking as if it might pierce his neck at any moment. His thin moustache wrinkled as his mouth bent in a frown. His dark eyes stared into Fincher's pale blue ones, which were as cold as ice.

"All right, Finch," he said. "Me and Cole and Giles went to the Clarendon Hotel like you told us to, braced old Mort Taggert to pay up, and he said he wouldn't pay no more. He said we done gone too far in killin' Hugh Pendergast. Said we was gonna pay for that. Said the old man, Harry, was goin' to get us, ever' one."

Fincher's eyes narrowed to icy slits.

"What did you say?"

"I told him we never killed nobody and walked out. But we watched the hotel and seen Pendergast come in and register at the desk. Cole went back in after Pendergast met that stage driver in the lobby, and they lit a shuck at the livery. Cole said Pendergast paid for three rooms. He made Taggert show him the register. I wrote down the names."

Carmichael pulled a scrap of paper out of his pocket and slid it across the table at Fincher.

Fincher read the names.

"Cole stayed behind to see who come to take them rooms."

"What names?" Abe asked Fincher.

"Pete Farnsworth, Brad Storm, and Harry Pendergast," Fincher said.

"Who in hell are they?" Abe said.

"Detectives, probably," Fincher said.

"That's what Cole aims to find out," Becker said.

"I know who they are," Fincher said.

"Yeah?" Carmichael said.

"They're trouble," Fincher said, and pushed the bottle of Old Taylor across to Carmichael.

In the quiet that followed, they could all hear the distant murmur of thunder, and the windows lit up like flash powder in a photographer's tray.

FIVE

Brad rode toward the smoke over rugged land that taxed Ginger's stamina. But the smoke was his only landmark, and he thought it might be the destination of the six men he tracked. Black clouds began to drift his way from the west, and he saw the latticework of lightning in their bulging muscles, felt the winds whirl and gust with increasing ferocity. The quail went silent, the hawks left the skies, and rabbits scurried underground. A sense of deep loneliness assailed him as he crossed the empty and broken land.

He looked at the western sky and thought of Felicity and Pilar, along with her husband, Julio, caught in the storm that must be raining down on his ranch, the cattle lashed by wind and rain, the horses neighing in terror at the thunder and lightning. He should be with them, he thought. Pilar was terribly afraid of storms and would be jumping out of her skin at every bolt of lightning, every peal of thunder. Felicity would be calm but worried about him, worried that he was on his way back home, caught in the storm, soaked to the skin. He wished he could project his thoughts to her and that she could hear his voice saying that he was all right and would be under shelter by nightfall, safe in the Clarendon Hotel.

But he knew she could not read his thoughts and that she would be worried about him until he showed up, safe and sound.

Brad shook these thoughts from his mind and rode Ginger over the undulating land toward the shawl of black smoke rising to the sky where the wind tore the clouds to shreds that evaporated like steam against the gray billows overhead.

And then the tracks appeared again, as if by magic, and he saw that they were leading to a jumble of buildings. He recognized them as part of a mining operation, and he circled to high ground above them and rode a parallel course to the horse tracks. Ahead, he saw a cut in the land that he knew was a road, and he headed that way. As he approached, he saw the buildings more clearly and knew he was looking at an old smelter, nestled in a bowl of cleared land, surrounded by low bluffs and rocky hills pocked with caves, and as he drew closer to the road, he could make out the tailings below the mine entrances, the green plants that had taken hold and grown out of the debris.

He saw a small horse barn and a pole corral, the main building with its stone chimney and a smaller, boxy building joined to it where the pale orange light from a lamp streamed through the windows. A man was rubbing down a horse outside the stable while another was pushing a wheelbarrow full of hay from a small building to the livery. Another man was pumping water into a trough.

Three men outside, he thought. Maybe another in the barn. And at least one in the smelting mill. How many in the lamp-lit room?

More than he could handle alone, he knew.

He rode across the road to the other side to see if there were any more outbuildings or perhaps men working one of the mines. He dismounted to get a better look. He tied Ginger's reins to a low bush and walked over to a small hill that blocked his view of the smelter.

The moment he stepped around the hill,

Brad knew he had made a mistake.

There, to his right, was a small building that resembled a blockhouse or a guard station. There were square openings on the sides and portholes for firearms on the side facing him. The door swung open, and two men stepped out.

The first man, a small, wiry individual wearing a long woolen overcoat, held a rifle in his hands. He also carried a pistol on his gun belt. The second man was slightly taller and heavier with a full graying beard, hatless, wearing a wool-lined jacket of worn leather. He wore only a pistol, but his dark eyes were oily, glistening like a wolf's under heavy brows. He worked a cud of tobacco in his mouth. His lips were wet and stained a sickly brown.

"Hold it right there, mister," the first man said, holding his rifle at the ready but not pointing it at Brad.

"Steady," Brad said.

"I'll steady you, pilgrim," the first man said, letting the rifle barrel fall a few inches. He was still not aiming, Brad knew, but he was getting ready to draw down on him. His finger was inside the trigger guard, but the rifle, a Winchester, was not yet cocked. "State your business."

Brad stared at the two men, assessing his

chances if either should open the ball.

"You better answer Ned here, mister," the second man said, "or you'll draw lead like a magnet." His right hand floated down to the butt of his Colt.

"What was the question?" Brad said, still studying the two men. They had feral eyes, but he saw no evidence that either of them had brains. Such men, especially when armed, were dangerous. They couldn't think past sourdough biscuits and whores, but they could act like the mindless hulks they were.

"I asked you what the hell you were doin' here," Ned said. "This here's private property."

"Oh, it is?" Brad said. "I didn't know."

"Well, you know now," the second man said.

"Shut up, Tom. I'm talkin' to this man."

Tom snorted.

"I was goin' to tell him to get the hell out of here," Tom said.

"I want to know what he's a-doin' here," Ned said. "You better answer me, mister." He lowered the barrel of his rifle a few inches.

Brad sensed that neither man was ready to shoot him in cold blood. They were guards, but probably had never shot a human being before. They looked like hunters, not man killers.

"I was hunting rattlesnakes," Brad said, in a clear, even voice that was almost audible.

"Huh?" Tom said.

"What's that?" Ned said.

"Rattlers," Brad said. "I saw two of them go right under that guardhouse yonder. Big ones."

Both men looked down at the ground, then at the stones under the corners of the guardhouse.

Brad slipped the rattles quietly from under his shirt, held them in the palm of his left hand so that they made no sound.

Ned looked up at Brad and lowered his rifle.

"Mister, you're full of shit," he said. "We ain't seen a rattler since we been here."

"Well, you just might, then."

"You ain't huntin' no rattlers," Tom said, lifting his gaze to Brad. "We'd a heard 'em if'n they crawled under the guardhouse. He's lyin', Ned."

"Yeah, I think you're right, Tom."

Ned brought the rifle down, aiming it at Brad's gut. Ned's thumb raised to a point just above the hammer.

Brad opened his hand. The rattles dropped. He shook the thong and the rattles crackled with sound.

Tom jumped backward. Ned's eyes widened and his thumb came to rest on the hammer of his Winchester.

Brad's right hand flew to the butt of his pistol, a blur of flesh so fast that Ned couldn't follow it or understand its meaning. Then he saw the dark bluing of the pistol's snout and his thumb pressed down on the hammer of his rifle.

Brad Storm cocked his Colt on the rise as he dipped into a fighting crouch.

He squeezed the trigger and the pistol bucked in his hand. It spewed flame and white smoke from its muzzle. The sound was like that of a cannon, and it was the last thing Ned heard.

Ned crumpled into a lifeless heap. His rifle slipped from his hand. His mouth gaped and his eyes frosted over in a dull wide-eyed stare into nothingness.

Tom recovered, and he clawed for the butt of his pistol.

Brad swung the barrel of his pistol, aiming at Tom's head.

"You bring that iron out and you're a dead man," Brad said.

Tom's hand froze in midair. He swallowed a mouthful of saliva.

Brad walked up to him and removed

Tom's pistol from its holster.

"You want to live, I take it," Brad said.

"Yessir, I surely do."

"Then you start walking. Real slow. You can tell the men you ride with that I'll be back."

"Who in hell are you? The law?"

"I'm your worst enemy," Brad said.

"What's your name?"

Tom still stood there, his hands half-raised, a look of puzzlement on his face. He looked as if he'd been kicked in the stomach. His breathing was shallow. His neck and forehead oozed sweat.

"They call me Sidewinder," Brad said.

"Sidewinder? Ain't no sidewinders in this part of the country."

"There's one."

"You?"

"Yeah, me."

"Then you ain't huntin' rattlesnakes like you said?"

"Oh, I'm hunting rattlesnakes all right. That's why I'll be back. You can count on it. Now get moving. Go on down to the smelter and tell your friends I mean business."

"You're outnumbered, man. I can tell you that."

"The more the merrier," Brad said and

stuck Tom's pistol into his belt.

Tom turned and walked around the guardhouse to a path that led down to the smelter. He still held his hands up like a man surrendering to an enemy.

Brad holstered his pistol and walked back to his horse. He mounted Ginger and headed for the road that would take him to Leadville. He put the spurs to Ginger and galloped out of sight of the guardhouse. Ahead were bulging behemoths of black clouds and the lancing streaks of lightning accompanied by the rippling roar of distant thunder. And against his face and body he felt the sweeping wind that already carried the moist promise of rain, the bone-chilling cold of the snowcapped mountains far beyond the advancing storm clouds that blocked the light from the sun and turned the day into night at high noon.

Six

Felicity Storm looked up at the darkening sky as she left the milking shed. She carried a large oak bucket in her left hand. The fresh milk sloshed against the sides of the wooden pail. The surface of the milk bubbled with foam, but she didn't spill any of it as she walked with quick, sure steps to the house. Pilar Aragon, Julio's wife, stood in the doorway, her aproned belly swollen with the child she was carrying.

Pilar reached for the handle of the bucket.

Felicity shook her head.

"No, Pilar. You must not strain yourself," Felicity said. She swung the bucket away from Pilar's grasp.

"You are too kind," Pilar said. "You make me feel useless."

Felicity swept past Pilar and set the bucket on the kitchen sideboard. The house was dark and felt oppressive to her.

"You could light a lamp for us, Pilar,"

Felicity said, surprised at her own irritation that had crept up unbidden to the surface of her mind.

"Por seguro," Pilar said. "Do you want the lamp in the front room lighted or the one in the kitchen?"

"The one in here," Felicity snapped. "There is no light in here at all."

Pilar waddled into the kitchen. The lamp on the table was barely visible. She walked to the sideboard.

"Where do you keep the matches?" she asked.

"They're on top of the stove."

She could have reached up and handed the matches to Pilar, but some perversity inside her, some unvoiced resentment against Pilar, made her stand there and watch Pilar strain to reach the top of the stove. It was not a good place to keep matches, as Brad often told her, but she preferred handiness over safety.

Pilar opened the matchbox and struck a match on the sandpaper strip. Then she lifted the glass chimney and touched the flame to the wick, turning the handle so that the wick rose from its berth. The lamp flared, and she pulled the match away and dropped the chimney back into place.

"Do you want me to make the butter?"

Pilar asked.

"Sit down, Pilar," Felicity said. "There, at the table. Let the milk settle."

Pilar sat down in one of the three chairs at the table. Felicity pulled one out and sat down opposite Pilar. Brad had told her not to have more than three chairs at their table. "One guest is enough for you and me," he had said.

"What if we have two guests for supper?" Felicity had asked him.

"I would discourage that."

"Why?"

"This isn't a stage stop. It's our home. Private. Just you and me."

"And an occasional guest," she had said with a trace of sarcasm in her voice.

"Very occasional."

The lamplight glinted off of Felicity's raven hair. She had brushed it to a high sheen. Pilar's black hair was dull and absorbed the light. Her thick braids hung over her shoulders and framed her large breasts like a pair of snakes. Felicity's hazel eyes glinted with gold and amber, a flicker of green light.

"You are very lucky, Pilar," Felicity said, looking at the pregnant woman's swollen belly.

"Why do you say this?"

"You have a husband to sleep with every night. You know where he is all the time. I am practically a widow. And I will not have a baby by a man who might not be in my bed when I wake up."

"But your husband will be back soon," Pilar said.

Felicity ignored Pilar's remark.

"I wash my husband's seeds from my womb when we sleep together. I do not want to have his child."

"But that is not right, Felicity. That is your duty. To give your husband a child, perhaps a son."

"No, it's not my duty. It's his duty to be a husband. Instead, he works for a detective agency. He is on a string, and a man in Denver, Harry Pendergast, just pulls it whenever he wants to."

"But Pendergast gave you money when you had lost the cattle. You were able to buy the cows, no?"

"Yes. Blood money. I thought Brad . . ."

Her voice drifted off, and Pilar looked at her quizzically, her black eyes glittering in the lamp glow, the faint rouge on her cheeks flaring a faint orange as she breathed through her nostrils. It was as if the twin snakes were hissing, Felicity thought.

"What did you think?" Pilar asked.

Felicity flattened both hands and held them at a level under the lamp so that Pilar could see them.

"Look at these," Felicity said.

Pilar looked at the backs of Felicity's hands.

"What do you wish me to see?" Pilar bent over the table until her eyes were a few inches from Felicity's hands.

"They're all withered," Felicity said. "Like an old woman's. I feel as if my whole body is going to dry up like old parchment, like a corn husk in autumn, and I'll look like an old woman, a sunbaked prune."

Felicity drew her hands away and clenched them into fists. "They were once beautiful," she said.

"They are still beautiful," Pilar said. "Rub them with butter or lard and the dryness will go away."

Felicity uncurled her fists and splayed her fingers onto the table. A sadness came into her eyes and flickered there like broken colored glass in a kaleidoscope.

"Underneath," she said, "they would be the same as now, old and shriveled like my aching heart."

"Your heart aches?" Pilar said, a tenderness and concern in her soft voice.

Thunder boomed overhead and lightning

stabbed the ground, lighting the windows with a startling flash. Both women jumped in their chairs; their bodies jerked into a stiffened sense of alarm. The peals of thunder rolled across the skies and faded into a black silence.

"For Brad," Felicity said when she had composed herself. "He seems so far away, even when he's here. Here at home. Since he hunted down and killed all those men, those cattle rustlers, he has changed into someone I no longer know."

"But you know him. You have love for him."

Felicity sighed and shook her head slightly.

"I love him, yes, but I don't know if he still loves me. He seems — oh, I don't know how to say it — distant, as if he and I lived in separate worlds. I hope it is not that way with you and Julio."

"No, it is not that way with me and Julio."

"Does — oh, I don't know how to ask this without embarrassing you — but does Julio, I mean does he, when you both go to bed together, want you as much as you want him?"

"It is equal," Pilar said. "He wants me as much as I want him. Is this not the way with your husband?"

"No. I must constantly entice Brad to

make love to me."

"What is entice?" Pilar asked.

"He seems not to notice my perfume or the lace on my nightgown, the way I purr when he comes close. Entice means something like setting out bait to catch an animal. I have to lure him to make love to me, and afterward I feel cheap, as if I've asked him for money so that he will lie with me."

"Perhaps if you do not chase him, set out the bait, he will chase you."

"No. He will ignore me and just go to sleep."

"I do not know what to say, Felicity. A man, a real man, like my Julio, has the lust in his heart. He wants me all the time. You know?"

"Yes, I know. It is good when Brad and I make love, but it is . . ." Felicity paused and took a deep breath as if searching for the words that would make Pilar understand.

"Yes?" Pilar said, waiting for the rest of it like a pupil in class when the teacher interrupts a story at a dramatic point.

"When Brad notices my perfume and tells me how nice I look, then I feel as if I have tricked him, that I have deceived him into making love to me. I feel like a very wicked woman."

"But that is not wicked, Felicity. That is what a woman does when she wants a man. Don't you know?"

"I know, I guess, but I wish, just once, Brad would pick me up in his arms, throw me onto the bed, and, well, have his way with me. I want to feel his lust, his desire, his power. I want to know that he wants me more than I want him. I want to surrender to him like a woman should surrender to the man she loves. I want him to take me again and again, without stopping. I want him to leave me soaked with perspiration and worn out, lifeless, at peace with the world and floating high above myself in a state of pure rapture."

Pilar reached across the table and touched Felicity's hand. She patted it.

"As a woman," she said, "you must take what you are given. You must love, and you will be loved. This is true."

Felicity shook her head, and that look of sadness crept back into her eyes. Then she closed them and began to weep. Her body trembled and her shoulders shook. She looked whipped.

"I can no longer accept the way things are," she sobbed. "Pilar, I'm so terribly lonely."

"But when Brad is here?"

"I'm still lonely. That's the trouble. And now I hate myself for telling you all this."

"Do not hate yourself, Felicity. You are a beautiful woman and you have much to give. Your husband will know this. He will see. He will love you as you wish to be loved."

The flame flickered in the lamp and the clouds seemed to envelop the house. Thunder boomed and lightning flashed all around, lighting every window, rattling every pane. Then the rain burst upon them, splashing against the windows, pounding the roof and blowing hard against the doors, striking all outside surfaces with the rattle and force of buckshot.

Felicity stood up and walked to the front window. She peered out and could not see the cattle or the grass, but only sheets of rain as dark as the black and empty meadow of her mind. She knew Brad would not come through this storm. He would not come to save her, to pull her out of her dark cave of despair and loneliness.

"I go home now," Pilar said. "Julio will be there by now."

"Yes, of course. Go," Felicity said.

Pilar opened the door, and the rain swept inside on the blasting wind. Felicity closed the door and latched it, soaked to the skin.

She stepped to the window and saw Pilar running to her house, past the milk barn, her shawl pulled over her head. She vanished into sheets of rain and was gone.

A crack of thunder drove Felicity away from the window just as the kitchen lamp ran out of oil and the flame died in the dry wick.

The house went dark and Felicity threw herself on the divan and wept in a sudden miasma of sadness that felt like a smothering cloak enveloping her very soul.

Seven

Mortimer Taggert, owner of the Clarendon Hotel in Leadville, was visibly nervous as he ushered Pete Farnsworth into his office. Pete noticed Deputy Sheriff Wally Culver standing just inside the doorway, looking through a peephole at the people in the lobby.

"He still there?" Taggert said to Culver.

"Still there, Mort. Only he's standing at the desk, looking at the ledger. He got up just after Pete checked in."

"What's going on, Mort?" Pete asked. "Where's Sheriff Dimsdale?"

"Didn't you hear, Pete? Dimsdale was shot to death a week ago on his front porch. Wally's acting sheriff for now. Wally, point out that man to Pete," Taggert said.

Culver stepped away from the peephole and Pete took his place.

"The hard case up at the desk," Culver said. "He's looked at that ledger after each check-in."

Pete looked at the man who was now staring at the door to Taggert's office, his eyes narrowed, his beard-stubbled jaw set hard, an unlit cheroot sliding back and forth in his mouth. He wasn't a big man, shorter than Pete, with slumped shoulders and a caved-in chest, a dirty bandanna sagging on his neck, an unbuttoned leather vest over his black-and-white checkered shirt.

"What's he want?" Pete asked Taggert.

"He's one of the men, one of that gang who barged in here this morning and demanded I pay them money every week. Two percent of what we take in."

"For what?"

"To stay open, they said. When I refused, they said I'd be sorry, that the Golden Council would see to it that I paid or died."

Pete stepped away from the peephole.

"Know his name?" Pete asked.

"I heard him called Cole by the other feller," Taggert said.

"His name is Cole Buskirk," Culver said. "I think he's one of the men who shot Sheriff Dimsdale to death, but I can't prove it."

"Sit down, boys," Taggert said. "I'm glad as hell to see you, Pete. Wally here is outgunned now that Dimsdale's dead and he's by himself. The other deputies quit after what happened to Dimsdale. Two dead sheriffs in less than a year. Both dead under somewhat mysterious circumstances."

Pete sprawled his lanky body in an upholstered chair and stretched out his long legs. Wally sat in a matching chair facing Taggert's cherrywood desk on which sat an inkwell, three quill pens, paid bills impaled on a metal spindle, a black ledger trimmed in red at the corners and spine, a stack of receipts in a small wooden box, three ashtrays, a briar pipe, and a small pouch of tobacco. On the wall there was a map of Colorado with leadville printed in large letters and black roads showing the distances between the major towns and some smaller ones, a tintype of the Clarendon, a portrait of George Washington, and a reproduction of the U.S. Constitution. There were no windows in the room, and one corner was taken up by a large, closed steel safe, a large captain's wheel positioned over the combination lock.

Pete looked at Wally.

"What can you tell me about this bunch, Wally? How do they operate? Do you know who the boss is? Mr. Pendergast told me the name of the man who killed his son, one Earl Fincher. He said Quince recognized his voice and that Earl and the others all wore yellow hoods."

"Earl rode shotgun on the stage for a while, with Quince," Wally said. "I guess he was learnin' the ropes. I don't know him, but Dimsdale said he was a hard case and to keep an eye on him."

"They call themselves the 'Golden Council,' " Taggert said. "If anyone refuses to pay protection money, a bunch of them wearing yellow hoods show up at the man's home and drag him out, beat him half to death, threaten to burn down his house, destroy his business. Generally, after a visit by the Golden Council, the men pay up."

"We don't know how many businessmen here are paying this gang," Wally said. "Most of 'em are afraid to talk about it."

"So, we know the names of two of them," Farnsworth said. "Cole out there and this Earl Fincher."

"There was another man with Cole Buskirk," Taggert said. "Don't know his name, but he left."

Pete looked at Wally with raised eyebrows.

Wally shrugged. "I didn't see him. I got here after he left."

"There's another thing," Taggert said.

"What's that?" Farnsworth said.

"I'm on the town council, and we had a

meeting last night to appoint a new sheriff to replace Dimsdale. I put Wally's name in the hat, but the president, Adolphus Wolfe, said we were going to hire a man named Alonzo Jigger."

"Who's Alonzo Jigger?" Farnsworth asked. He looked at both Taggert and Culver.

Culver cleared his throat.

"After Mort told me about it, I looked through our wanted posters and dodgers, and there was an old one with a small reward for Alonzo Jigger out of Pueblo. Two hunnert dollars, I think. No likeness on the dodger."

"What was the charge?" Farnsworth asked.

"Embezzlement."

"Hmmm," Farnsworth murmured. "Very interesting. What do you make of this Jigger?"

"Supposed to take over as sheriff tomorrow," Culver said. "Never heard of him."

Pete looked at Mort Taggert as they all heard the faint stutter of thunder. They could also hear the wind swirling around outside and slapping the wooden frame of the hotel.

"Anything else, Mr. Taggert?"

"Why, yes. I tried to bring up this Golden Council thing, and the other board members, including Wolfe, said it was none of our business."

"What exactly was said?" Pete asked.

"Adolphus said there was nothing illegal about men selling insurance policies. He said that's all they were doing. None of the others had ever heard of men wearing yellow hoods and using intimidation."

"Insurance policies?" Farnsworth said.

Taggert picked up a document, handed it to Farnsworth.

"Cole Buskirk gave me this when he and that other man first came into my office this morning."

Pete read the document.

LOBO SURETY COMPANY was printed out in bold letters across the top. It seemed to be written in legal terms and offered insurance against robbery, fire, and all other calamities that were not acts of God for the sum of two percent of the signee's gross income per week.

"This is outrageous," Farnsworth said.

"It's extortion," Taggert exploded, pounding a fist on his desk. "Downright extortion."

Culver smiled wanly as the sound of thunder grew louder. The door to Taggert's office rattled slightly as the wind followed a patron into the hotel.

"I expect we can get to the bottom of this," Farnsworth said. "I expect to have another detective check in sometime this afternoon or tonight."

"Brad Storm?" Taggert said.

"Yes."

"Mr. Pendergast has a permanent room here for him and you, Mr. Farnsworth."

"Call me Pete."

"I heard of Storm," Wally said. "Ain't he the man who busted up that gang of cattle rustlers last year? Him and you?"

"The very same," Pete said. "Good man."

"Why do they call him 'Sidewinder'?" Wally asked.

"Long story," Pete said, and rose to his feet. "I left my kit at the stage stop. I'll be up in my room when Storm gets here, Mr. Taggert."

"I'll send him right up, Pete."

Pete smiled.

He leaned over and shook Taggert's hand. Then he walked over to Culver.

"Wally, are you afraid of this Golden Council?"

"No, I reckon not."

"Good. Then we may need you to help us round them up."

"I'm ready to help."

"And I want to meet this new sheriff as

soon as possible. Tomorrow, you say?"

"That's when he's supposed to take over."

Pete stopped at the door and turned around to look at Taggert.

"What's the name of that banker again?"

"Adolphus Wolfe. He owns the Leadville Bank and Trust. Why?"

"Just curious," Pete said and left. He saw no sign of Cole Buskirk in the lobby. He stopped at the desk and rang the bell. A clerk emerged from a small room.

"Yes, sir, Mr. Farnsworth, what can I do for you?"

"Where'd that man go who was here a few minutes ago?"

"Oh, he left. Went outside and got on his horse. I saw him ride off."

"Thanks."

He saw the black sky light up as he looked out the window. There wasn't a soul on the street. A few lamps burned in some of the windows. They cast yellow light onto the boardwalks.

It looked, he thought, like a ghost town.

Eight

Brad rode Ginger a few yards above the blockhouse and turned left to look at the other side of it. It was a small frame building made of whipsawed lumber that had lost its paint and weathered to a dull gray under the onslaughts of wind, rain, snow, and blowing sand. There was a small tin chimney on one side of the sloped roof, its opening covered by a piece of tin bolted on above it in the shape of a Chinese coolie's straw hat. There was probably room inside for a cot or two, a table, and a couple of chairs, he thought. And next to the building was a half cord of wood and a box full of kindling. Likely they had a potbellied stove to keep the occupants warm in cold weather.

He turned and saw that the blockhouse had a good view of the road behind him, clear to the top of the grade where it disappeared. When he looked down at the smelter, he could see Tom walking with slow steps toward the entrance some four hundred yards away. In the basin where the smelter buildings stood sprawled out, he saw adobe houses, probably built for the hard-rock miners and mill workers. There were a dozen, at least, some with lighted windows, others crumbling along their sides. There could be dozens of men housed in the compound, Brad thought, perhaps more. And at one end of the bowl, the slate black waters of a creek wound in a half circle before it vanished below the compound. There were no ripples in the water, and it looked deep enough to last all year round. There was a small earthen dam and a ditch leading to the smelter, sloped so the water could run inside the mill through a square opening in the main building.

He wondered if he should have boasted about his return to face so many men.

There was no sign on the smelter's walls or on its roof. He thought that it must be one of the first to be built in and around Leadville, perhaps before the original settlement of Oro City had been founded and named.

He emptied the cylinder of Tom's pistol and dropped it to the ground before he turned Ginger in the direction of Leadville.

Tom had not yet reached the halfway

point between the blockhouse and the old abandoned smelter. Brad topped the slope leading down to the basin and took to the wagon-rutted road.

Facing him, to the west, huge black thunderheads hid the mountains. He saw occasional lances of lightning that lit jagged pathways through the clouds, and moments later he heard the muttered murmurs of rolling thunder, so faint he could barely hear them above the creak of saddle leather.

He shivered in the tidal wave of cold that washed over him, a cold borne on the beating wings of the wind that preceded the oncoming storm. He did not know how far it was to Leadville, but his senses told him that it was probably no more than five miles. And he was sure that this road he was on, fresh-tracked with three sets of horseshoes heading west and two heading back to the smelter, would take him where he needed to go. Those tracks told a story, but he did not know the whole of it. Three men rode into town. Two rode back.

He felt a slight twinge in his left hand. He turned it over and looked at the fleshy part. That was where the sidewinder had bitten him, and there were two flesh protuberances where the snake's fangs had punctured his flesh. The healed-over wounds acted up when the weather changed and were a reminder of his close call with death. And of the Hopi who had saved him, nursed him back to health — the same Hopi who had cut off the rattles and strung a leather thong through the wide end. The same set of rattles he now wore around his neck. Gray Owl had since gone back to his own country, back to the land of the sidewinders. And somewhere up in the deeps of the mountains, his good friend Wading Crow, who had let him witness the Snake Dance taught to him by Gray Owl, was summering with his Arapaho tribes people, still free.

Brad rubbed the twin moles on his hand and the itch subsided. He topped the rise and rode into broken country. It was odd how fast the land could change in the foothills. The road was not visible for long stretches, but followed the contours of the broken land, through gullies and arroyos, over humpbacks and rugged knolls. Maybe, he thought, it was more than five miles to Leadville. There was no way to tell because the black clouds had sunk even lower in the sky and blocked his view for many miles. He had to imagine the Rockies, for they were now hidden, their brawny muscles tickled by forks of lightning and the shrouding rain a thin scrim beneath the clouds, a ragged curtain dripping from the bowels of the thunderheads.

And then Ginger's ears stiffened, twisted right and left, a pair of cones. The horse had heard something or smelled something. Brad rode on, down into a shallow gully, his right hand resting on the butt of his Colt, his senses sharpened to a razor's edge. Ginger made a low sound in his throat, and then the horseman appeared over the edge of the gully, riding a steel dust gray.

Brad reined Ginger to a halt and waited as the man approached.

"Howdy," Cole said. "You must be Jig. That right? Finch said you might show up today."

"Yeah," Brad lied. "I didn't catch your name."

"I'm Cole Buskirk. I'm the man who got you the vacancy." Cole snickered as he said it.

"Vacancy?"

"Yeah, you're going to be the new sheriff in Leadville. Right?"

"Right," Brad said.

"Well, didn't Earl tell you? I put that bald-headed bastard Rodney Dimsdale's lamp out. You ought to have seen it, Jigger. I shot him on his front porch just about dusk. A clean shot to the head. His brains flew out like custard, and blood poured all over his shirt, as red as his damned suspenders. He never knew what hit him. He dropped like a sack of meal right off his porch."

"Good job," Brad said, feeling a sickness inside his belly, a revulsion that rose up in him like an angry cougar, all claws and fangs. He had known Dimsdale and liked him.

"So, you'll be the new sheriff, Jig. Or should I call you Alonzo?"

"Jig is fine."

"Should make it easy for the Golden Council from now on with you sittin' in Dimsdale's chair."

"How far is it to Leadville?"

"Oh, maybe three, four miles from here. I just left the Clarendon. You got a detective snoopin' around. I saw him check in. Name of Pete Farnsworth. I can't wait to tell Finch."

"Well, you better get crackin', Cole. Looks like we're both going to get wet before this day's over."

"Yeah." Cole stood up in stirrups and turned around to look at the sky, but he couldn't see how close the rain was from inside the gully. "I'll tell Finch and the boys I seen you, Jig. I surely will."

"You do that, Cole," Brad said.

The two men passed each other. When Brad looked back, Cole was waving goodbye as he rode out of the gully.

It was a good four miles to Leadville by Brad's reckoning. A long, hard four miles, mostly uphill, and when he saw the low buildings of town, his heart raced. He had now identified two of the men who rode with Earl Fincher, the man who had killed Hugh Pendergast. He knew their faces and their names. That was a start, at least.

He wondered what the Golden Council was. Was that the name of Fincher's gang or a company they all worked for? Well, maybe Pete Farnsworth would know what it meant.

By the time he rode up to the livery stables, it was nearly pitch-dark and he felt the first spray of rain on his face. He put Ginger in a stall and took his bedroll and saddlebags with him. By the time he emerged from the livery and started walking to the hotel, patters of rain were dimpling the dry, dusty street and there was not a soul to be seen. Thunder rumbled all around him, and the buildings rose up out of the darkness in shivering, blinding light as bolts of energy threaded the clouds.

"Yes, sir, Mr. Storm," the clerk said. "Here's your key. Mr. Farnsworth was in his room, but is now back in Mr. Taggert's office. Through that door right there. They're expecting you. You can leave your bedroll and saddlebags with me, and I'll have them sent up to your room."

"Much obliged," Brad said and headed for the door with the sign MANAGER over the name MORTIMER TAGGERT. He knocked.

"Go right on in, Mr. Storm," the clerk said, and Brad opened the door.

The three men in the room all stared at him. He recognized Taggert and Farnsworth, but not the other man, who wore a deputy sheriff's badge.

"Brad," Pete exclaimed as he pulled his lanky form up out of the chair, his legs and arms at all angles like a scarecrow's form in the wind.

"Well, who were you expecting?" Brad asked, a wide grin on his face. "Alonzo Jigger?"

Taggert's face went blank and turned the color of pasty oatmeal. Pete's jaw dropped, and Deputy Wally Culver's eyes turned black as he squinted in disbelief.

"Huh?" Culver harrumphed.

Pete walked up to Brad and shook his hand, looking him over.

"I don't know where you been, Brad, but you been somewhere for sure. You didn't get that name from Harry or Quince."

"That's right. But I tracked down the men who killed Hugh. I've been to the dragon's lair, Pete, and we've got our work cut out for us."

"What do you mean?" Pete asked.

"I mean we're not dealing with four or five men."

"How many?"

"I don't know, but there's one less than there was before I rode up on their camp."

"You had a gunfight?"

"That's a mite dramatic. I ran into two guards, and one was a little fidgety with his rifle. I got the drop on the second one and sent him packing. By now, I'm sure Earl Fincher knows I'm here, and he damned sure knows you're here."

"How?"

"I also ran into a man named Cole Buskirk who thought I was Alonzo Jigger. He called me 'Jig,' and I didn't tell him any different."

Pete swore.

"Won't you sit down, Brad?" Taggert said. "It appears we have a lot to talk about." Taggert waved Storm to a chair.

"By the way, Brad, this is Deputy Wally Culver. I don't think you two have met."

"You worked for Sheriff Dimsdale, I

gather," Brad said.

"Sure did. I'd like to get my hands on the man who killed him."

"I know who killed Dimsdale," Brad said after he had shaken Culver's hand and sat down. "It was all I could do to keep from killing him."

"What?" Pete said. "You —"

"He's alive, like the other man I let go, because I want Fincher to get a taste of something."

"A taste of something?" Taggert said.

"Fear. I want him to get a taste of fear before I kill him."

The room went silent, but they could all hear the lashing rain on the roof and the sides of the hotel building. And they could all hear the ominous growl of thunder and the crackle of lightning as the sky opened up in a drenching torrent of rain.

"The gods are angry," Pete whispered to himself.

But the others all heard him, and Wally nodded like a true believer.

NINE

Alonzo Jigger stood before the magistrate, Dewey Leffingwell, at nine A.M. the next morning. Jigger raised his right hand. His left hand rested on a copy of the Holy Bible held out by Judge Leffingwell's clerk, Emmett Rooney. Witnessing the swearing-in ceremony was Deputy Sheriff Wallace Culver. Brad Storm and Pete Farnsworth sat in a pew watching the brief ceremony, which was held in a small courtroom that had once been a warehouse for mining equipment.

A shaft of wan sunlight poured through a small window. Dust motes danced and sparkled in its pale glow. The room smelled musty after the night's heavy rainfall, as if it had been locked away from the weather for a number of years. A push broom stood silently in one corner, unused for a week, and in another corner stood a mop and pail, both dry as desert sand. A rim of light outlined the door to the judge's chamber, the black lettering on the door illegible.

"Do you solemnly swear to uphold the laws of the State of Colorado and the City of Leadville, so help you God?" Leffingwell intoned.

"I do," Jigger said.

"And to defend this city and state against all enemies?"

"I do."

"Then I hereby appoint you, Alonzo Jigger, sheriff of Leadville."

Jigger dropped his right hand and the judge shook it. The clerk pulled the Bible away and tucked it under his arm.

Leffingwell removed a badge from his pocket and pinned it on Jigger's chest, just above the left-hand pocket of his shirt. Then he shook Jigger's hand again. Wally Culver stepped up and also shook Jigger's hand.

"Welcome to Leadville, Sheriff Jigger," Wally said.

"Call me 'Jig,' Wally," Jigger said, a mirthless swipe of a smile on his face. He was a small, nondescript figure of a man with a bland face that looked as if it had been sculpted from a bowl of month-old mush, a tiny hooked nose with a large mole on its tip, swooping sideburns that flared to his chin, and a shock of wiry red hair streaming from under his black hat. He wore his striped wool pants tucked into his boots, and carried two .38 Smith & Wesson pistols with mother-of-pearl grips on his silver and black gun belt. He looked, Brad thought, like a comic character from one of Shakespeare's stage plays, with his black shirt and buttons like a breastplate on his small chest.

"What do you think?" Pete whispered to Brad as he leaned close to Brad's ear and held a hand up to shield his mouth.

"Not much," Brad said and stood up. Pete got up, too, and the two men started for the door.

"Hold on, gentlemen," Jigger called, and the two men stopped.

Jigger walked up to them, Wally a few paces behind.

"I don't believe we've met," Jigger said. "And I like to get to know my constituents."

"Constituents?" Brad said as Jigger stuck out his hand.

"The townfolk who are in my care." Jigger had a high-pitched, squeaky voice and what sounded like a Virginia drawl. "I'm Jig."

Brad just stood there, but Pete took Jig's hand and shook it up and down once in a perfunctory gesture.

"Pete Farnsworth."

"Ah, with the Denver Detective Agency," Jig said. "I am familiar with your name."

"How so?" Pete asked.

"I went through all of the major cases handled by my two late predecessors and saw your name and association." Jigger turned to Brad. "And you, sir? Who might you be?"

Jigger held his hand out to Brad.

"I might be anybody, but my name's Storm."

"Ah, Brad Storm, I presume. I never forget a name. And are you also a private detective in the employ of Harry Pendergast?"

"I'm a cattle rancher," Brad said.

Jigger's eyes narrowed to twin slits, then widened with a sudden quickness that was startling.

The judge and the clerk left the room, closing the door to the chamber behind them.

There was a stillness in the room, and the shaft of sunlight wiggled with dust motes that resembled moths or midges flying helter-skelter in a tawny sky.

"Funny," Jig said, "Dimsdale's records indicate that you were instrumental in breaking up a gang of cattle rustlers. Killing every man jack of them, I might add, and that Mr. Pendergast hired you on as a private detective."

Brad said nothing.

Jigger's eyes narrowed again. Just for an instant.

"So, you are not on the Denver Detective Agency's payroll, Mr. Storm?"

"I don't know if I am or not."

Jigger looked at Pete, his eyebrows arched to reveal the question in his eyes.

"Why the interest, Sheriff?" Pete said. "We just came to see you sworn in. Wondered what kind of man the city had hired."

"In order to keep the peace, I must question everyone I deem suspicious."

"And you're suspicious of us?"

"Not you so much, Mr. Farnsworth, but this man who calls himself a rancher is a little bit off his range."

Pete opened his mouth to speak, but Brad put up his hand to stop him.

The motes evaporated and the sunlight made a pale pool on the hardwood floor like a urine stain.

"Mr. Pendergast asked me to look into the murder of his son, Hugh," Brad said. "I'm a private detective in his employ, for the moment. That answer your question, Sheriff?"

Jigger rubbed one of his sideburns. It sounded like a finger brushing a piece of sandpaper.

"So long as private detectives don't interfere with my duties as a legitimate lawman, I see no reason why we can't get along, Mr. Storm."

"Our duties are every bit as legitimate as yours, Mr. Jigger," Pete said.

"Call me Jig, Mr. Farnsworth. I hope we can become friends."

"Well, Jig, are you going to investigate the murder of Hugh Pendergast?" Pete's jaw hardened as he peered deep into Jigger's brown eyes.

"I'm not accustomed to discussing my investigations with private detectives."

"Is that a yes or a no?" Brad asked.

"I saw no formal complaint on my desk in the sheriff's office. And I have yet to meet the senior Mr. Pendergast. So, for the moment, my answer is no. The young man's murder might lie outside my official jurisdiction."

"Hugh Pendergast lived in Leadville," Pete said. "He worked for a local firm. He was murdered on his job. I would say that falls within your jurisdiction, Sheriff."

"That remains to be seen," Jigger said. Then he walked to the door, brushing the two men aside.

"Gentlemen," he said and walked out onto the muddy street.

Wally stood there, a look of uncertainty on his face, as if he wasn't sure where he was or what he should do.

"I-I guess I better go with him," he said to Pete, his look changing from uncertainty to apologetic.

"Well, he's your sheriff, Wally," Pete said.

"Gawd, he's a hard man," Wally said. "He don't look like a sheriff, but he sure knows how to needle a man."

"Not like Dimsdale, eh?" Pete said.

"No. Rodney was a lot more polite, and he didn't treat people he just met like they were criminals." He paused, then started for the door. "I got to go," he said.

"Watch yourself, Wally," Pete said. "From what Brad tells me, Jigger is one of the Golden Council."

"I-I'll keep my eyes open."

"Watch your back at the same time," Brad said.

"I surely will," Culver said and stepped outside onto the boardwalk. He left the door open, and the sounds of the street filtered into the courtroom: the squeak of a wagon wheel, the yap of a dog, the grunt of a hog, the chatter of two women down the street, and the squishing thump of a horse's hooves on wet ground.

Pete and Brad stepped outside. Pete

closed the door. They walked a few paces on the drying boardwalk and stood under the overhang of a store that sold kitchen utensils.

"Well, what do you make of Jigger?" Pete asked.

"He sounds somewhat educated and might know something about sheriffing. But there's something oily about him, something devious hidden in those clown clothes he wears."

"You have a good eye, Brad."

"I'd say Jigger is a very dangerous man."

"Maybe. Why?"

"He doesn't look like a sheriff. He doesn't act like a sheriff. Yet he now wears a badge. That makes him dangerous. And there's something else."

"What's that?" Pete pulled out a sack of tobacco and a packet of cigarette papers. He offered them to Brad, who shook his head. Pete took one of the papers and crimped it between his thumb and forefinger.

"Whoever those men are at that old smelter, they want something from this town. Maybe more than money. And they're willing to go to any lengths to get it. Even sending a man to act as sheriff. Maybe to shield them."

Pete filled the trough of thin paper with tobacco, pulled the string tight with his teeth, plopped the bag back in his pocket, and rolled the paper into a cigarette. He licked the exposed edge and put the end into his mouth.

"What's worth more than money?" Pete asked as he probed in his pocket for a match.

"Power. Somebody in this town wants power, someone bigger than Earl Fincher or Alonzo Jigger. Someone who's smarter than the whole bunch put together."

"You really believe that?" Pete struck the match on the sole of his boot and lit his cigarette.

"After seeing Jigger, more than ever. And I think that Golden Council is a little high-toned for a bunch of gun-slicks hiding out in an old abandoned smelter. I think — Well, it doesn't matter."

"No, go on, Brad. What you say interests me." Pete blew out a plume of blue-gray smoke, which the breeze shredded and wafted away in tatters above their heads.

"A name like that sounds almost like . . . like a holy crusade or a grand alliance of some kind."

"Yeah, I see what you mean. Kind of. Well, how are we going to get this Earl Fincher under lock and key and bring him before the judge?"

"I don't know, Pete. Maybe we have to smoke him out, or trick him some way. You and I can't just go up against the whole bunch of them."

"No. We'd need a small army to attack the men in that smelter."

"First, I think we ought to find out more about the Golden Council. Talk to some of those who are paying protection money to the gang. If we find out how it works and who's heading it up, we might be able to pick them off, one by one."

"All right," Pete said. "Let's start asking some questions. Let's see if we can't get some coffee at that little café over by the hotel. I think the owner paid somebody to stay in business."

The two men walked to the corner and crossed the street on a path that had been trampled so much it was nearly dry. Pete smoked his cigarette, but Brad was studying every person he saw, male or female, as if they might be a threat.

After meeting Jigger and two of the men who worked for Earl Fincher, he was suspicious of every stranger.

That was against his nature and not a good feeling at all.

TEN

Earl Fincher didn't take his hat off when they buried Ned Crawford at the far end of the barren plain. Some of the men showed respect and held their hats in their hands while Ned's corpse was rolled into the four-foot-deep hole that four of them had dug. Dick Emsley poured a sack of lime into the grave. Then he and Lenny Carmichael shoveled the pile of dirt onto Ned's lime-covered body. Tom Ferguson wiped away a tear, then all but Finch covered the mound of dirt with stones they had gathered from around the grave site.

"Everybody," Fincher barked. "Meeting in ten minutes. And I mean everybody. Emsley, you get those bars and set 'em on the table."

Dick nodded and beckoned to Abe Danner. The two men picked up all the shovels and started back to the main building ahead of the others. Fincher glared at Cole, who stood by the grave in a solemn state, his head bent, eyes closed.

"Cole, you walk back with me. Now." There was iron in Fincher's voice, and the words cracked against Cole Buskirk's ears like the metal tips of a quirt.

The other men scattered to their adobes with nearly ten minutes to kill.

"What's on your mind, Finch?" Cole asked as he walked up to Fincher.

"You know damned well what's on my mind, you dumb bastard."

"Hell, I thought it was Jigger, comin' from the smelter like he was."

The two men started walking toward the smelter. The ground was drying after the rain. The wind was up and warm under the yellow glow of the morning sun. Their boots crunched on the gritty surface that had already lost its moisture. The rainstorm had been heavy but had not lasted long. Now the sky was clear with only a few cottony clouds floating in an azure sky.

"Now you know better since you met the real Jigger last night. The man you saw was probably the same man who killed Ned. Hell, it was the same man. I want you and Ferguson to take the silver into town and then start looking for that man."

"Sure, Finch."

"You both got a real good look at him."

"Yeah, a pretty good look," Cole said.

"He's probably still in Leadville. After you take the silver to the bank, you start lookin'. And I've got a list of new customers I want you both to call on."

"Customers?"

"That's what the boss wants us to call them from now on. Now that Jig's the sheriff, the boss wants everything to look real legal."

"Who is the boss, anyway?" Cole asked.

"That ain't for you to know just yet."

"I thought you was the boss, Finch."

"So far as you and the other men are concerned, I am the boss. But there's a bigger chunk of gold behind what we do. And you'll hear more about that in our meeting this morning."

"I can't wait," Cole said.

"Don't give me none of your smart mouth either, Cole. You're on a short string as it is."

"How come? I got a look at one of them fellas Pendergast got a room for. Farnsworth checked in and went right into the office with that Deputy Culver and Mr. Taggert."

"You shot your mouth off to that bastard you met on the road. Now he knows more than he's supposed to about Jig. And now he knows who killed Dimsdale. That was your biggest mistake. You put your own neck in a noose with that, Cole."

"Hell, it was an honest mistake."

"It was a dumb mistake. Now, see if you can't make up for it and find that bastard. You might even save your sorry neck. Whoever that bastard was, he probably tracked us to our hideout from where we stopped the stage. Abe backtracked him a ways just before that storm hit, and he sure as hell came from someplace up on the Denver road."

"What do you want us to do with him, Finch?"

"Kill him," Fincher said as the two reached the smelter.

Fincher's tone seemed to come from a deep black sepulcher where the only light boiled up raging from the fires of hell. Cole felt Fincher's hot breath on his face, a breath fetid with garlic and night whiskey.

"All right, Finch," Cole said, stepping back a pace. "I'll find him and kill him."

Fincher looked past Cole to the gaping holes of the mines in the sedimentary rock that was streaked with dark smears from the storm runoff of the day before. The caves were grim reminders of other men's failures and the earth that would someday remove all traces of men's folly. The adobe huts would crumble, the smelter would collapse and blow away, and his own grave would have no tombstone. But now, for the time he lived, he would take everything life had to give and kill any man who stood in his way. Like Jig, he had spent five years in a Yuma prison, where he saw cruelty and viciousness up close and met men who laughed at the law and their misdeeds under the lash of sadistic guards with malicious grins on their faces.

Fincher knew how the world was, and how it had taken Clarabelle from him. He was bound to take what he wanted from it, and spilling other men's blood was a way to pay back those men who had tried to steal his soul.

"Who's up in the blockhouse?" he asked Cole as he took his gaze away from the rocky bluffs beyond the creek.

"Al Loomis and Seth Vickers."

"Walk up there and tell 'em to come down. I want everybody at this meeting. Shake a leg."

"Sure, boss," Cole said and started off at a lope to the guardhouse up on the rim of the bowl.

Fincher went inside the main building, walked through pale beams of sunlight, stirring up dust motes that wriggled like the ghosts of fireflies in the gloom.

Emsley and Danner were just entering the room. They carried a board laden with the silver bars they had remelted and stamped.

"Just set the bars on the table," Finch said. "Leave the board for now."

He walked over and picked up one of the bars. It glistened in the feeble light that streamed through the window. He examined the engraved lettering and smacked his lips in satisfaction.

The initials embedded in the bar were "GC" and there was a small outline of a wolf just beneath it.

"Very good," he said and put the bar back on the two-by-twelve table.

"Payday," Abe said.

Dick Emsley grinned.

"It'll sure give us a taste," Fincher said. "A taste of richer days to come."

His eyes glinted with the dark ice of greed and the surety of more riches to come when the Golden Council grabbed Leadville by the throat and they all ruled over it like kings.

That was the dream. That was the message he would deliver this morning to the men who were loyal to him, handpicked every one, and every one as greedy for money and power as he was.

"Today," he told Dick and Abe, "we take charge of our destiny. We were once pushed by Fate, trounced and kicked and beaten back by the world. But now, we take charge and leave Fate to the fallen, to the unworthy, to the shopkeepers and merchants. We are the force for change, and by all the gods, we will succeed."

Abe and Dick stared at Fincher and saw in his eyes the burning flames of the fanatic, the unmistakable mark of a true leader. This was a man they could follow, and the proof of his genius lay on the table shining with the same light the stars beamed down to Earth.

The silver was like a magnet, Fincher thought, and it imparted power and wealth to those who possessed it.

He felt powerful and alive, more alive than ever.

And the silver was only part of the proof he needed that he would not fail in his mission.

Nothing could stop him now.

Nothing.

ELEVEN

Holly Danner put an arm around Wilma Crawford's shoulder and gave her a squeeze.

"I'm real sorry Finch wouldn't let you pay your last respects to Ned. He didn't want any of us women to see Ned buried."

The two women stood in front of one of the adobe huts, their laundry baskets on the ground in front of them. They were waiting for the other women to walk with them to the creek where they would do their washing. They could not see where the men had gone with Ned's body because it was on the far end of the basin, well beyond the old smelter.

"It's all right, Holly," Wilma said. "I just wonder why they didn't bury him over yonder where I could see his grave from my window."

She pointed to a small cemetery beneath a rocky outcropping below one of the abandoned mines.

"Did you ever walk through that graveyard?" Holly asked.

"No. I've been afraid of graveyards ever since I was a little girl in Shreve's Port."

"I read the boards," Holly said, "most of 'em rotting away, but you can still read the names. Most of 'em what's buried there are women or young girls. Oh, a boy or two, and some men, but mostly women our age, in their twenties or early thirties."

Wilma looked over at the graveyard. There were a few crosses still standing, but most of the markers were flat at the top end of the small mounds. She shivered in the freshet of breeze and pulled her shawl more tightly around her shoulders. The sky was a pale blue with little streaks and puffs of clouds floating serenely overhead.

She was a skinny waif of a woman with straggly blond hair, a small nose and mouth, and a wizened look of age on her young face. There were pockmarks on her cheeks, reminders of a childhood disease that had taken her little brother and sister back in Louisiana. She was only twenty-three but looked forty in her faded print dress and high button shoes with both heels worn down on the insides. She was slightly bowlegged but so short that it was barely noticeable except when she walked. She wore no stockings or makeup, but her arms, legs, face, and hands were tanned by the sun.

"Well, it's no wonder those women and children died out here," Wilma said. "Havin' to live in these 'dobes summers and winters, with the flies and the rats and the other horrible critters."

"It is hard," Holly said. "Some nights we just lie in our beds and look up at the ceiling and watch the lizards lick up the flying bugs. One night a lizard dropped its tail right on Abe's chest. I screamed and Abe just laughed."

They saw the men come back from the burial. One of them walked up to the guardhouse but was too far away for the women to identify.

"Look," Wilma said. "They're all going into the big room at that smelter."

"Abe said they might have a meeting this morning. He said Finch was in a rage over Ned getting killed."

The prairie sun hung like a glowing yellow disk in the eastern quarter of the sky, and Holly pulled her bonnet lower on that side of her face.

"They're always having meetings," Wilma said. "And Ned hated to be up in that guardhouse. He said he felt like a sewer rat trapped in the bottom of an outhouse."

"Little good it did for them two to be up there on guard."

"It didn't do Ned no good," Wilma said.

Two of the other women approached, carrying their clothes baskets on their hips like sidesaddles. One of them, Myrtle Ferguson, was smoking a cheroot, the fumes floating in front of her in a thin stream of bluish-gray fog. The other, Fanny Becker, was waddling along beside her with a lump of chewing tobacco bulging out her cheek. They were chattering away like magpies, their bonnets pulled low over their foreheads to block out the sun.

"Good morning, girls," Fanny said and spat a stream of tobacco onto the ground. "Either of you got the matches?"

"I do," Holly said. "You bring the lye soap?"

"I sure did," Fanny said, waddling up to them on stout fatty legs.

Holly and Wilma picked up their clothes baskets and joined in the small procession as they headed for the creek.

"I think Delia and Elaine are already at the crick," Myrtle said. "A couple of addle brains, you ask me."

"Oh, Myrtle, you shouldn't say such things," Holly said.

"Well, it's true," Myrtle said. "I never saw

a pair so downright dumb as them two."

"They're just slow and unschooled is all," Wilma said.

"You stop that kind of talk, Myrtle," Holly said. "It ain't kindly to make fun of the dumb."

Elaine Emsley and Delia Vickers were both gathering firewood. They had stacked twigs and dry brush next to three shallow pits, each encircled by stones, and were walking back to the creek, their arms laden with more burnable sticks gathered from the prairie beyond the basin.

There were three small ore cars lined up over the fire pits, rusted by rain and blackened by flames. The women had carried each one to their washing spot, pushing and pulling the heavy iron carts from where they had been stacked near one of the mines alongside piles of narrow-gauge track, broken picks, and shovels. A fourth cart stood apart from the others and was used for rinsing the washed clothing.

"Creek's running fast this morning," Elaine said as she dumped her firewood next to a pit.

"All that rain last night," Delia said as she stooped to unload her own kindling.

"I see it," Holly said as she set down her bundle in its wicker basket. "We'll have to be careful."

"You fall in," Delia said, "and you'll be gone in a twinklin'." Her smile was radiant. She was a dark-haired woman with dazzling blue eyes. Her long hair was gathered up in a bun at the back of her head. She was slim and graceful, but the lines in her face testified to a hard life.

Elaine was a buxom blond woman with a boxy face, drooping jowls, and ears that stuck out like cup handles. She was thick in the waist, but had surprisingly slim legs that she kept neatly shaven with her husband's straight razor. Her eyes were a soft light brown that seemed to change color with her moods.

There were grates on the bank that the women used for scrubbing their soapy clothes and each woman began to carry her clothes over to the creek and pile them next to the grates.

"Who's got the soap?" Delia asked as she carried a bucket of water to the first ore car. She didn't expect an answer and didn't get one.

Each of the women began to fill buckets with the fast-running creek water and filled the cars.

Wilma set some brush under the cars and packed them tight.

"Put plenty of sage on each one," Fanny said. "I love the smell of burning sage."

Myrtle lit the fires, careful to keep her face away from the flames as she blew on each spark until it caught fire.

"Where's Winifred?" Elaine asked Holly.

"Oh, she's sick," Holly said. "I went to get her this morning, and she was still in bed."

"She's been tryin' to kill that baby in her belly for a week," Delia said.

"Well, there were a lot of bloody rags by her bed when I saw her this morning," Holly said.

"Maybe she got rid of the little bastard," Elaine said and laughed.

Wilma looked sick and had to gulp in air so she wouldn't throw up her breakfast.

The fires burned, and the women set to washing their clothes by the creek, passing the bar of lye soap back and forth, scrubbing on the grates and carrying their washed clothes to the ore carts for rinsing.

The creek water was ice-cold, and the women stopped often to rub their hands or warm them at one of the fires. Their hands blanched from the exposure and turned rosy from the caustic burn of the lye soap. Their fingers ached and trembled from the chilly waters of the creek.

The women chattered and gossiped,

sweated and fanned their faces as the sun rose higher in the sky and grew hotter by the minute.

An hour later, Winifred Loomis trudged up, lugging a basket full of clothing, along with blood-soaked rags and towels. She panted from the effort as she set her basket down. Her face was drawn and flushed. Her brown hair hung straight down. She looked weak and her plump legs shook as she closed her eyes and drew in deep breaths.

"Your belly's gone, Winnie," Elaine remarked. "You drop your kid?"

Winifred nodded, too worn out to speak.

"Boy or gal?" Myrtle asked.

"Myrtle, what a terrible question to ask," Fanny said.

"Boy," Winnie said and began to weep.

Holly left her washing and rose to her feet. She walked up to Winnie and put an arm around her.

"There, there," she said. "It's all right. Myrtle didn't mean anything. She was just curious."

"I know. I just couldn't bring up a kid out here, livin' like we do. It's just too hard. Too goddamned grim."

"Now, now, Winnie, don't you worry. It'll be all right."

"I buried it in the cemetery," she said.

"Next to another little boy."

"I'll help you wash your clothes," Holly said. "You just sit down and rest."

"Eat some red meat," Elaine called out from the creek. "That'll give you your blood back."

"What do you know about it, Elaine?" Myrtle said. "You're as barren as a barn door."

"Hey, you little bitch," Elaine started to say.

"Both of you, stop it," Delia said. "Let's all bow our heads and close our eyes for a minute over that little lost boy of Winnie's."

Holly helped Winnie sit down and then carried her basket to the creek.

"They're all gone," Winnie said, after a few minutes of quiet among the other women. "Al come back to get his rifle and bedroll."

"All the men?" Wilma asked.

"Yes. All of them rode out just as I was leavin' to come down here."

"Where are they going?" Myrtle asked.

"To Leadville. Al said they were goin' to hunt down that feller what killed your man, Wilma. He said they was goin' to kill someone named Sidewinder."

"Sidewinder?" Wilma said.

"That was the name he used."

Wilma shuddered.

"It sounds like some kind of snake," Elaine said.

"Yes, I think it is," Holly said. She began to dip a bloody towel in the rushing creek water.

"Sidewinder," she said to herself and started looking all around as if expecting to see a rattlesnake slither up to them. She shuddered and then splashed cold water on her face.

The women were quiet for several moments, each wondering what kind of trouble lay ahead.

"No one in the guardhouse?" Elaine asked after a while.

"No," Winnie said. "They all left. Even Fincher."

"Looks like we better get our pistols out and load our shotguns," Delia said. "Just in case."

"Just in case what?" Elaine said.

"In case that Sidewinder rides in and tries to rape all of us."

Elaine started to laugh, but the solemnity of the other women made her cut it short.

"You'd like that, wouldn't you, Elaine?" Myrtle said, her voice laden with sarcasm.

Elaine gave Myrtle a dirty look.

And then it was quiet again as the sun rose

ever higher, crawling up the arc of the blue sky like some flaming eye beating down on them, streaking ribbons of gold and silver through the tumbling waters of the creek.

TWELVE

The gaudy sign over the entrance to the café featured a single word, CACTUS, framed by a pair of painted prickly pear cacti, bold caricatures of the real plant. Pete Farnsworth led the way through the wooden door on which hung a sign in two languages: OPEN and ABIERTO.

Brad followed Pete to a table in the far corner of the main room. There was an adjoining room that was darker and not as crowded. The clink of plates and silverware could be heard under the drone of conversations in both Spanish and English. The tables were inlaid with colorful tiles in red, green, and yellow, with salt and pepper shakers in the center, along with a clay ashtray.

"Smells good," Brad said.

"The food is good here."

They both looked up at the blackboard behind the counter where two waitresses attended to the customers seated there.

"Hungry?" Pete asked.

Brad shook his head.

"Just coffee," he said.

"You had breakfast?"

"I never eat before I go out hunting," Brad said.

Pete smiled.

A pretty young waitress came to their table. She wore a small green apron trimmed in yellow, a red skirt, and yellow blouse. She carried a small slate and a piece of chalk. She had high cheekbones and a thin patrician nose over a small delicate mouth. The vermilion pigment in her cheekbones spoke of her mixed blood: part Spanish, part Indian.

"You want the coffee? Breakfast? Lunch?"

"Two coffees only," Pete said. "Black."

The young lady nodded and did not write it down on the tablet.

"And I would like to see the owner."

"Eh?"

Brad wondered if she had not understood the English word.

Pete pulled a small tablet from his pocket, turned a page and read the name.

"Ernesto Valencia," he said. "I want to talk to him."

"Ernesto, *sí*," she said. "He is in the office. I will tell him to come."

The young woman walked through the opening in the counter and emerged a moment later from the small office, a man following in her wake. While she bent down to retrieve two cups and place them on the back counter, the man approached Pete and Brad. He looked to be in his late thirties, with flecks of gray in his sideburns and moustache, his straight black hair cut short and dyed, slicked down with pomade. He wore a faded striped shirt and tight black trousers. His shoes were polished to a high sheen.

"You asked to see me," Valencia said in crisp, barely accented tones.

"Sit down, Mr. Valencia," Pete said and introduced himself and Brad Storm.

Ernesto pulled out one of the wooden chairs cut from a barrel and cushioned in the seat. The three men shook hands.

Pete reached into his shirt pocket and pulled out a miniature wallet. He opened it to display his badge. Ernesto looked down at it. Pete closed the wallet and slipped it back into his pocket. The room hummed with the animated conversations of women and a few old men who did not work. The women were either maids or housewives out for a morning of shopping with friends. For many, the café served as a listening post and gossip exchange, or constituted their only chance for a social life.

"Brad and I are private detectives," Pete said. "We work for the Denver Detective Agency."

"Police?" Ernest said.

"Policía privada," Pete said.

"Ah," Ernesto said, his dark brown eyes wide. "And what is it you wish to talk to me about?"

"The Golden Council," Pete said. "Insurance."

Ernesto's eyes seemed to darken to black onyx, and his mouth went slack beneath his moustache.

"I pay it," he said. "Every week."

"How much do you pay?" Pete asked.

The girl set two cups of steaming coffee in front of Brad and Pete, looked at Ernesto.

"*Café,* Ernesto?" she said.

"No," he said, and she backed away with polite movements.

Brad blew on his coffee and took a sip. Pete stared at Ernesto.

"How much each week, Ernesto?"

"Two percent of the money I take in," he said.

"Who comes to collect the money?"

"Two men. Never the same. I do not know

their names. They do not tell me their names. But I pay." He paused. *"Cada semana,"* he said bitterly.

"Why do you pay these men?" Pete asked and picked up his cup, the steam rising in tendrils to his nostrils.

The morning sun blazed through the front windows of the café, the light fracturing and transforming into different colors from the painted legends of meals and prices. The faces of the women seated at the front tables took on orange, blue, and green complexions.

"Because," Ernesto said, closing his eyes for a moment. Sweat broke out on his forehead and he reached for a handkerchief in his back pocket. He rubbed the cloth across his forehead and swiped the wrinkles in his neck that were taking on a glistening sheen from the perspiration.

"Because?" Pete said.

"I do not wish to talk about this. I pay the insurance. Why do you ask?"

"I think these men are *bandidos,*" Pete said. "I also think they killed Sheriff Brown and Sheriff Dimsdale. They may have killed others who would not pay for their insurance. If these men, these criminals, threatened you in any way, we want to know about it. We want to bring these men to justice before the court."

Ernesto's whole body seemed to wince as he listened to Pete's words. His face contorted into a mask of remembered pain, and Brad thought he was going to cry at any moment.

"My friend," Ernesto said in a low voice, looking around to see if any eavesdroppers might hear him, "was one of the first these men came to see. He owned a small *tienda* on Calle Flores. He sold the little rugs and the clay pots, the *ceniceros* and the big *ollas* his wife and family made in their home. It was a very small business and Eladio Camarillo did not make much money except when it is summer.

"That is when two men came to him, this last summer, and told him they wanted money every week. He told them he could not give them the money. They told him he would be sorry and they went away."

"And that was it?" Pete said.

"Oh, no, that was not the end of it. Maybe one week later, Eladio was awakened by a noise outside his house and there were four or five men on horses. They came into his house and they molested his daughters and his wife, Marianna, and they told him he must pay every week or they would kill his family and burn down his house."

"Did he know who the men were?" Pete asked.

Ernesto shook his head.

"They had no faces. They wore the yellow, what do you say, hoods? Yes, the hoods. They raped his woman and his two daughters and they beat Ernesto's face before they rode away."

"So, what did your friend do?" Pete asked.

"He paid the two men who came to see him the next day. He paid them until he had no more money and then he moved away to Pueblo."

"Are there any others you know of who are paying and have not moved away?" Pete drank from his cup and swished the coffee around in his mouth.

"Yes, there are others."

"Will you give me their names?"

"I do not know. They are very afraid of these men after what happened to Eladio and his family."

"It would help us if we could talk to them."

"I will think about it. Maybe you will come back tomorrow, eh?"

"We'll be back," Pete said. "Thank you."

Ernesto arose from his chair and bowed slightly.

"Enjoy the coffee," he said in Spanish.

"And you do not pay me. I hope you will not tell what I have told you."

"I don't remember your telling me anything," Pete said.

Ernesto smiled a half smile and returned to his office. He spoke to the serving girl first and pointed at their table, waving a finger to show her that she was not to give Pete and Brad a bill.

Brad swallowed a gulp of coffee, a look of deep reflection on his face.

"We've got to get those bastards," Pete said.

"Well, Pete, we know where they are. Do you have an army at your disposal?"

"How many men would we need? How many could you get to ride with us to that smelter?"

"Just Julio and Carlos, who work for me. That gives us three."

"I hope you're not laughing about this."

"No, Pete. I'm not laughing. That man is genuinely afraid. And I don't blame him. This Golden Council will stop at nothing to achieve their ends. They pick on poor shop owners and Ernesto here. But if they are allowed to keep doing this, they won't stop until they've hog-tied the whole town."

"They must be stopped. You agree?"

"I agree, but there's something else that

bothers me about this gang."

"Oh? What is that?" Pete drank the rest of his coffee and waved away the serving girl when she came toward them carrying a pot in her hand.

"Somebody pretty smart is heading this outfit. And I think it's somebody we wouldn't expect right off."

"I don't get your drift," Pete said.

"From what little I've seen of these hooded gunmen, they're not smart enough to run an insurance agency, much less keep track of sales figures."

"I think I see what you mean, Brad."

Brad finished his own coffee, set his cup down.

"It's that two percent that I wonder about."

"What?"

"Why two percent? Where does that come from? Not from those boys in the yellow hoods. They wouldn't have the brains and they would probably take all they could get and leave town."

Pete leaned back in his chair and pushed his hat back on his head. He looked at Brad with a newfound respect.

"You may be on to something, Brad. I hadn't thought about that. I just thought they were pretty well organized. And for them to murder Hugh, it showed me they don't want anybody in their way."

He stood up, and Brad pushed away from the table.

"I think we have to look for the real boss of this outfit," he said. "I'll give it some more thought. But you'll be on your own for a few days."

"How come?"

"I expected to be home last night. I'm riding back to the ranch today. I'll see to the stock and talk to Felicity. Be back in a day or two."

"Promise?"

Brad shook his head. "In this uncertain world, Pete, any man who makes promises is a damned fool."

"I'll look for you when I see you, then."

"That might be best. I'll get back as soon as I can."

"Bring your ideas with you, Brad."

"I will, and I'll bring this, too," he said, lifting the rattles from his shirt for a brief moment.

"Ever the Sidewinder," Pete said, stepping away from the table into a splash of sunlight.

"You bet," Brad said. He reached into his pocket, pulled out a two-dollar bill, and pushed it under his cup. Then he started for the door. The serving girl smiled at him, and Brad touched a finger to the brim of his hat in farewell.

Thirteen

Earl Fincher led his men from the basin over the uphill road, the sun at their backs, the breeze in their faces. The mountains stood out like majestic monuments, clear and distinct in the crisp morning air. An hour later, he called a halt.

His men gathered around him in a semicircle, their horses pawing the ground, switching their tails at the gray deerflies, snorting and bobbing their heads.

"Here's where we split up in twos," he said. "You all have places to stay while you're in Leadville. Lenny and I will bunk up at the Carmody over on Pine Street, by the river. You have your assignments. I want every Mex shopkeeper and store owner signed up for our protection services."

The men laughed.

"That hotel stinks," Emsley said.

"No more'n yours, Dick," Earl said, and the men laughed again.

"I especially want each of you to pay attention to the lists of names I gave you. Them what is suspected of being money hoarders get special attention. I circled them on your lists. If there's anything we hate, men, it's Mexes hoardin' money."

The men snickered in understanding.

"That money they're hoarding belongs in the bank." He paused. "Or in our pockets."

The men all laughed again and looked at each other with knowing smirks on their faces.

Leather creaked as the men shifted their weights in the saddles. The restless horses pawed the ground.

"You all have your hoods?"

The men all nodded. A couple of them grunted in the affirmative.

"Abe, you, Vickers, Giles, and Dick, pay a call on that little weasel Sanchez tonight. He turned us down, and I want the fear of God put into him."

"We ought to hang that Mex," Vickers said. "He said he'd never pay us one centavo."

"We'll see what he says tomorrow after you boys put the boots to his wife," Fincher said.

"I'd like to put the boots to him," Abe said.

Some of the men laughed.

"I mean —" Abe started to say.

"We know what you mean, Abe," Earl said. "You don't like your pussy on a stick."

All of the men guffawed at Fincher's joke.

"Tonight," Fincher continued, "Lenny and I will meet up with Al Loomis and Cole and pay a call on Mr. Mortimer Taggert and his wife at their home. Al, meet us at the livery around midnight."

"Taggert will never pay," Tom Ferguson said. "He's as stubborn as a Missouri mule."

"And," Cole said, "I think he's the one who called in that Denver detective, Farnsworth."

"I have no doubt. That's why we're goin' to read Mr. Taggert chapter and verse tonight."

"You gonna kill him?" Cole asked.

"We won't have to," Fincher said.

"Cole, you and Tom go straight to the bank when you get to town and put those silver bars in the safe-deposit box. You got 'em wrapped right?"

Cole and Tom both nodded.

"Ain't we goin' to draw on them bars?" Tom asked.

"That will be taken care of, Tom. In due time," Fincher replied.

"I hope so. At seventeen bucks the ounce —"

"Never mind about the price of silver. Just do what you're told," Fincher said.

"Sure, boss."

"Then you and Cole make some calls on those holdout Mexes on your list."

"We know what to do, Finch," Cole said. "You don't need to keep harpin' on it like my old lady."

Nobody laughed. Fincher frowned and looked up at the sun to mark the time of day. He held a hand over his forehead to shade his eyes.

"Okay, men, split up, two by two, head into town from different directions and at different times. I know where you all are stayin', and we'll go over tonight's business tomorrow. Meantime, you boys see how many Mexes you can get to pay up on their insurance premiums this afternoon."

"That it?" Vickers said. His horse was restless and fighting the bit. He whapped the dun on its withers to calm the gelding down.

Fincher reached in his pocket. He pulled out a large golden coin.

"No, there's one more thing. I got a fifty-dollar gold piece here. It goes to the man who puts a bullet in that Sidewinder feller."

The men all murmured in approval.

"Fifty bucks to kill a human snake," Fincher said, holding the gold piece up and showing it to all of them. "So keep your eyes peeled. Now wear out some leather gettin' to town. Cole, you bring me a receipt for that silver." Fincher slipped the gold piece back in his pocket with a dramatic flourish. He could almost hear the men mentally licking their lips.

"Sure thing," Cole said.

Lenny and Finch rode off to the north while the others split up in preplanned pairs and took different paths to Leadville.

Mountain quail called and a hawk skimmed over the road, its head turning from side to side as it hunted for its next meal. A lone coyote slunk into the brush on padded feet, a ghostly shadow in the sage and creosote. A lizard slid across a rock, the sun illuminating its blue and yellow stripes, its nervous tail.

In moments, the road was empty and the sun boiled at its zenith, a furious cauldron of ignited gases and orange flames belching from its furnace.

FOURTEEN

Brad could smell the livery stable half a block before his boots took him there. There were horses tied outside at the hitch rail, unsaddled dray horses, and the false front that proclaimed, in fairly fresh paint, LEADVILLE LIVERY STABLES was still damp from the previous night's rain. The faded letters ORO CITY were still faintly visible underneath the new paint in LEADVILLE.

Flies sawed the air around the horses' rumps, and several of the big draft horses had blood trails down their flanks where the buzzers had fed. Some of the horses wore the brand Circle PM on their hips.

He walked into the darkness of the stable, his nostrils filled with the fresh scent of manure and urine. He set down his bedroll, saddlebags, and rifle just inside the door and looked down the shadowy corridor of the livery. Every stall was filled, it seemed, and he walked toward the back doors where

Ethan Sommers, the stable master, pushed one of them open a crack. He put his shoulder to the door since the outside was bucking against a muddy curl of dirt and offal that blocked the door's base.

"Morning, Ethan," Brad said and helped the young man push the door wide. The back lot was still wet with pools of water steaming in the sun. The two pushed the other door open, and sunlight streaked the straw floor of the stable just inside and pushed the shadows toward the center of the building.

"You here to pick up Ginger?" Ethan asked, the stub of an unlit cigar between his rotting teeth. He never smoked inside the livery but chewed up a half dozen cheap cigars a day until he went home or to the nearest cantina. He was a lean whip of a man in his midtwenties who wore faded overalls and a blue bandanna around his neck, a moth-eaten silk jockey's cap on his head, a reminder of earlier days before both of his legs and hips had been broken in a fall from a Kentucky Thoroughbred in Frankfort.

"Yeah," Brad said to Ethan as the man limped toward Ginger's stall. "I can saddle him."

"You can saddle him, Brad, but you can't

ride him. I ain't opened the tack room yet. Last night's rain flooded my crick and I got here late."

"What do you mean I can't ride him?"

"Ginger threw a shoe this morning when I grained him. You aimin' to ride back to your ranch, horse'll come up lame before you go ten rod."

Brad swore under his breath.

"Show you, if you want to see," Ethan said. "Or I can get your tack."

"Show me."

The two men walked to Ginger's stall. Ethan opened the gate. It was dark inside, like the inner sanctum of a coal bin, but Brad could see the bare outlines of his horse. Ginger whickered at him, but made no move to come out.

"You wait here, Brad," Ethan said and slipped a rope halter off a nail on the post in front of the doorjamb. He stepped inside, spoke in low tones to Ginger, and emerged seconds later, leading the strawberry roan by the halter. Ginger's blaze was slightly smudged from rubbing up against the walls of the stall.

"It's that left hind foot," Ethan said. "I got the shoe in a box of knickknacks in the tack room."

"Usable?" Brad said as he took the rope

from Ethan and patted Ginger on his withers.

"Worn to a nub on one side. Couldn't no way pitch with it even."

"Damn," Brad said as he bent down to lift Ginger's left hind leg. There was no shoe on it.

"Better check them others, too. You might be due for a full shoeing."

"You're not a smithy," Brad said.

Ethan laughed, a dry crackle in his quivering, tremulous throat, and shifted the cigar stub to the other side of his mouth.

"In my time," he said, "when I was about eight years old, back in Kentucky, I shoed all our horses while my old man stood over me with a hickory switch. Ain't had a hankerin' for shoein' since I first rode at the county fair."

"No, I guess not," Brad said. He stood up straight. "I suppose it's a country mile to the nearest blacksmith."

"Used to be," Ethan said. "Feller name of Sanchez opened him a shop right down the street. Was an old furniture store there, but the owner went broke and the building come vacant. Sanchez is a good smithy. I send him all my business. Like right now, he's got some draft horses from the Panamint lined up needing new shoes."

"Wonder if he can fit me in. I'm in kind of a hurry to get home."

"He might, if you grease his palm and tell him I sent you."

"I'll walk Ginger down there," Brad said. "I got a four-hour ride ahead of me."

"Yeah, you live way back in the hills, don't you?"

"I live so far back I have to cart the sun in with a wheelbarrow every morning."

Ethan laughed.

"And it's all uphill," Brad said.

"It's a good twenty miles. I hunted elk up there last fall and seen your herd."

"That's right," Brad said. "Felicity poured hot coffee in you until I was scared you might drown."

"That was one cold mornin'," Ethan said. "I can get that shoe for you if you want to take it to Ruben's."

"Sure. That the smithy's name, Ruben?"

"Yeah. Ruben Sanchez. Got him a pretty little wife, I think." He walked toward the tack room. "I'll get you that shoe."

"I'll walk Ginger down there if you point me in the right direction." Brad was trying to remember a furniture store being on the same block as the livery. It seemed to him that there was a man running some kind of shop where he could hear the lathe spinning, the ripping sound of a whipsaw, and the sound of a blunt iron hammer on wood. An old German guy, if he recollected right, fuzzy white beard all over his face, a bald head so shiny it blinded a man when he stood outside his shop in the sun. Yes, he remembered the place.

"Whatever happened to old Grunig?" Brad asked when Ethan returned with the badly worn shoe in his hand. "Otto, wasn't it?"

"Yeah. Otto Grunig."

"He die?"

"Nope. He packed up one day a couple of months ago, moved to Cherry Creek or Littleton, somewhere up by Denver."

"Business bad here in Leadville?"

"Naw, Otto was doin' all right. Least I think he was. He said he wasn't goin' to pay no insurance to thieves."

"You pay insurance here?"

"Hell, I don't own the place. Lemuel Foreman does. And yeah, he pays insurance. Two percent of what we take in ever' week, he says."

"You know who he pays that money to?"

"He told me it was some outfit called the Golden Council."

"You ever see any of the, what do you call them, collectors?"

"No, they don't come by here, 'cept to put up their horses. I think Lem just makes his payment over to the bank."

Brad took the shoe and stuck it in his back pocket. It was thin on one side and bent out of shape.

"What bank, do you know?"

"Leadville Bank and Trust, over on Main."

"I know where it is," Brad said. "Thanks, Ethan."

"Just turn right when you go out," he said as Brad led Ginger toward the front doors. "Same direction as the smithy. You can't miss it."

Brad raised a hand and shook it behind his back and over his head.

"I know where it is," he said again.

He walked Ginger out into the street and past the horses at the hitch rail. There was a saddle and bridle shop next door, then a small flower shop where they also sold clay pots, seeds, latticed arbors, bags of fertilizer, wood trim, and gardening implements. Then a small vacant building that had once been a furniture store.

The sign on the small false front read BLACKSMITH, R. SANCHEZ PROP.

There were three horses tied to hitch rings set in concrete in front of the shop. These had the same brand as those at the livery,

Circle PM, owned by the Panamint Mining Company.

Brad tied the halter rope to an empty hitch ring and walked inside through the wide double doors. He smelled the smoke and the red-hot iron and the sweat of horses. He saw a small man bent over a forge, holding a horseshoe in one hand and pumping on a bellows with the other. The shoe glowed a fiery orange on one side, and black smoke poured from the forge in curlicue spirals. The blacksmith wore smoked glasses and a black skullcap made out of heavy leather.

He wore an old Colt Navy .36-caliber pistol on his belt that had been converted from cap-and-ball to percussion. The belt was shiny with brass bullets.

"Mr. Sanchez," Brad said when he walked up behind the blacksmith.

Sanchez whirled around and clawed for his pistol. He let the shoe drop into the shortened barrel of water and pushed his dark glasses up on his forehead.

Brad shot out a hand and gripped Sanchez's wrist.

"Whoa there," he said. "I come to have you shoe my horse, feller."

Sanchez relaxed.

"You a-scared me," he said in a liquid

Spanish accent.

"Didn't mean to. Can you shoe my horse?" Brad pulled the worn and bent shoe from his pocket and showed it to Sanchez.

Sanchez shook his head.

"I got four horses to shoe right now," he said.

"I know. Ethan told me. I'm in a real hurry. I'll make it worth your time."

Sanchez, a diminutive, slat-thin, clean-shaven man who looked to be in his late twenties, with skin the color of old cowhide and a broken nose, heaved a sigh that sounded like a thin version of his bellows.

"I don't know. I got one in here, and more outside, and some still up at the livery." He pointed to a large black horse in the back of the shop. It stood hipshot in front of a chute, much like a man waiting to get into a barber's chair.

"Five dollars gold if you can get me mounted in a half hour," Brad said.

Sanchez stuck out his hand.

"I am called Ruben Sanchez," he said. "I will make your horse the shoe. Bring him inside."

"Thank you," Brad said.

"Five dollars. It buys much of the rice and beans."

Ruben's grin was infectious and Brad

smiled back.

"I appreciate it," he said and started to go outside to get Ginger. He stopped and turned to Sanchez.

"Who did you think I was when I came up behind you?" he asked.

It seemed to Brad that all the blood drained out of Ruben's face. He turned away, picked up the tongs, and retrieved the shoe from the water.

"No importa," he said in Spanish. "It does not matter."

But Brad knew that it did matter. It mattered a hell of a lot. He looked at the old pistol on Ruben's gun belt. Ruben shrugged.

"That iron can get you in a lot of trouble," Brad said.

"Or keep me alive," Ruben said.

FIFTEEN

It was not just by chance that Pete Farnsworth saw Cole Buskirk and Tom Ferguson ride into Leadville and head straight for the Leadville Bank & Trust.

He had been watching the bank before it opened, writing down in his little notebook what he observed. He saw, for instance, the first person to open the bank, a man he took to be the janitor since later Pete saw him sweeping the flowered walkway to the entrance. And there was a woman, a couple of men he took to be clerks, and, finally, a portly man in a double-breasted pin-striped suit that might have come from Brooks Brothers in New York, who wore both spats and a derby hat and carried a straight cane with a gold or polished brass head on it.

The man, Pete was sure, was the owner of the bank, Adolphus Wolfe. He also carried a small leather briefcase and had arrived in a fancy sulky drawn by a sorrel gelding with a star blaze on its forehead and four white stockings. The driver of the sulky was a Negro man dressed out in fancy livery, including a silk top hat, white vest and bloodred shirt, dark blue trousers, and shiny black boots.

After Adolphus Wolfe entered the bank, the driver turned the sulky around and drove it down the street in the direction from whence it had come. Pete was sure the black man would return at the bank's closing time.

When the restaurant across the street from the bank opened before noon, Pete walked over and took a seat outside at a table with a large umbrella over it that provided both shade and a modicum of concealment. The restaurant was called Chez Paris and was owned by a Frenchman from New Orleans named Pierre Brevert who had come to Colorado as a prospector, made enough money to realize he would die poor before he was forty years old, and so opened a restaurant because, as he said, "Men must eat." He put on French airs and did speak a kind of French patois, but all he knew about France was from reading Victor Hugo, Gustave Flaubert, and Émile Zola. He was the self-educated son of a French thief and a Creole woman who had once been his father's favorite whore. He made a decent living as a restaurateur, but employed male Mexican waiters and a Chinese cook who provided him with opium to smoke.

Pete did not know Pierre but knew something about him. He didn't like the man, but the food at the Chez was good and the coffee, Arbuckles, even better.

He ordered a light lunch of crêpes suzette stuffed with boiled beef, sliced *pommes frites,* and a boiled egg, with coffee. He made notes in his tablet and continued to watch the front of the bank. Shortly after noon, while he was still eating, he saw two riders approach. They tied up their horses at the hitch rings in front of the bank and dismounted. He recognized one of them and wrote his name down in the tablet.

Cole Buskirk.

Pete's blood quickened as he saw the two men go to their saddlebags and extract two bundles each. The bundles appeared to be burlap sacks wrapped around their contents.

Pete left five silver dollars on the table and walked across the street. The man who was with Buskirk dropped one of the bundles just as Pete came up behind him.

Buskirk turned at that moment and looked down at the burlap sack.

"Tom, you dumb sumbitch," he said.

Tom bent down to pick up the sack, but he grabbed it by the wrong end. The sack unraveled as he picked it up and its contents spilled out onto the ground.

Pete's eyes widened as he saw the silver bars glistening in the postnoon sun.

"I'll help you," Pete said, leaning over to pick up one of the bars.

"Hey," Tom said and reached for the bar.

Pete snatched it away and stood up.

"You," Cole said before he could think, and Pete stared him down.

"Just helping the man," Pete said as Ferguson grabbed the open end of the burlap sack and began pushing the silver back inside.

Pete turned the bar over in his hands, looked at all sides of it.

"Give it back," Ferguson said as he stood up, his face flushed from the effort.

"Some silver bars were stolen from the Leadville Stage about a week ago," Pete said. "These look an awful lot like them."

"They ain't them," Buskirk said.

"I can see that. These bear a different stamp than the Circle PM."

"What's it to you?" Ferguson said, stretching out his arm, his hand turned palm up in a beseeching gesture.

"What's GC stand for?" Pete said.

"None of your damned business," Buskirk said. "Hand him back that bar."

"Is that a wolf's head underneath?" Pete asked.

"He done told you it was none of your business, mister," Ferguson said and lunged for the bar.

Pete stepped back and pulled the bar back with him, out of Ferguson's reach.

Ferguson began to sweat. Perspiration glistened on his forehead. He was juggling two sacks, and the open one hung down from one hand like a sack of potatoes, while the other seemed to be slipping from his grasp.

"Farnsworth," Cole said, "this ain't none of your business. Now, give Tom back that chunk of silver or I'll draw down on you."

"I'm investigating a robbery, Buskirk," Pete said, "and I have every right to examine this silver bar or any others you might have in your possession."

"Them bars ain't stole," Ferguson said, his face drenched with sweat.

"Tell me what the GC stands for, Tom," Pete said.

He shifted the bar to his left hand and let his right hand drop to the butt of his pistol.

Ferguson looked at Buskirk, as if to say he was helpless and didn't know if he should answer Farnsworth's question.

"Golden Council," Cole said, a look of hatred in his eyes. "Now give it back."

"You work for the Golden Council?" Pete said to Cole.

"I ain't answerin' no questions."

"What about you, Tom? You a member of this Golden Council?"

Ferguson's eyes seemed to beg Cole to tell him whether to answer Farnsworth's question or not.

"Cole, what are we gonna do?" Tom said.

"Go get the sheriff if he don't give that bar back to you in two seconds," Cole said.

"Sheriff Jigger?" Pete said. "I might go get him myself."

Cole glared at Pete, his lips crunched tight, his nostrils flaring with rage.

"If I put these bags down, Farnsworth, the next thing I'll do is draw down on you and blow your sorry ass plumb to hell."

Pete smiled and handed the bar back to Ferguson.

"Here," he said. "We wouldn't want any gunplay right here in broad daylight, would we?"

Ferguson grabbed the bar and slid it into the open sack. His lips quivered in relief, and he heaved a heavy sigh.

"Come on, Tom," Cole said. "We won't

have no more truck with this bastard."

Tom turned and walked to where Cole was standing. He wrestled with the awkward sack of silver that dropped under the weight of the bars.

"I'll be seeing you, Cole," Pete said as the two men headed for the front doors of the bank. "You can bet on it."

Cole didn't answer. He and Tom disappeared into the bank, looking like robbers going the wrong way.

There was a paper banner stuck against one window of the bank that Pete hadn't noticed before.

WE PAY HIGHEST INTEREST ON SAVINGS, it read. And, in larger type: 2% PER ANNUM.

Pete wrote that down in his notebook and walked back to the restaurant. He sat at the same table that had been cleared. When the waiter came by, he said, "I didn't finish my coffee, Paco. Can you bring me a fresh pot?"

Paco nodded.

Several minutes passed while Pete sipped his coffee.

Cole and Tom emerged from the back. They were now carrying empty burlap sacks. Cole was stuffing a receipt into his shirt pocket. He looked all around before he walked to his horse behind Tom.

"Yeah," Pete murmured to himself, "you

can bet I'll see you again, Cole Buskirk."

He took out the makings and began to roll a cigarette.

He wondered if he should follow Cole and Tom. No, he decided. Leadville wasn't that big of a town. When the time came, he could find them.

It was that bank sign that intrigued him at the moment.

Two percent per annum. That's what the bank paid in interest on savings accounts.

That, he thought, was mighty interesting.

SIXTEEN

Ruben snubbed Ginger up to a freestanding post and patted the horse's neck. He had already straightened the shoe Brad had brought him and found a matching size among the blank shoes hung on nails driven into one of the walls of his shop. He walked behind Ginger and backed into the horse's left hind leg, lifting his bare hoof. He took a curved knife and began to trim the hoof where it had frayed after the shoe was thrown.

"Good horse," Ruben said. He put the knife away and pulled the new shoe from his leather apron pocket. He placed it against the hoof and examined its fit.

"You're pretty good at that, Ruben. You have a good eye."

"Sometimes I am lucky."

He dropped Ginger's hoof and reached over to a small keg filled with horseshoe nails. He selected several and put them in his mouth, points facing outward. Then he picked up a small hammer, backed into Ginger's haunch again, lifted the hoof, and fitted the new shoe to its contours. He drove a nail partway into the hoof through the top center hole.

" 'Skilled' is the word I would use," Brad said.

"What is 'skilled'?"

"Good at what you do."

"I do this to make the money," Ruben said. "When I do not shoe horses, I make the iron figures." He looked up and pointed to a dark corner in the rear of the shop. Brad saw several wrought-iron sculptures. One of them was a man with a helmet and a spear in one hand. He resembled a drawing Brad had seen of a Spanish conquistador. There was another one of a fat man on a small fat horse. They were like stick figures drawn on paper except that they were made of iron, and he could feel the power in their fluid lines, the energy in their complex designs.

"A man with a spear," Brad said. "Pretty good."

"That is Don Quixote," Ruben said. "And the fat one on the donkey, he is Sancho Panza. I will make a windmill next."

"I know the story," Brad said. "What's

your story, Ruben?"

"Eh?"

"You don't pay the insurance to the Golden Council. Did they threaten you?"

"They say I will be sorry that I do not pay."

"Are you afraid of them?"

"I have the pistol. I have fire to throw in their faces if they come back."

"These are dangerous men, Ruben."

"They are *cobardes,* how do you say, 'cowards,' I think."

"Cowards, yes. But cowards do not come at you face-to-face. They sneak up behind you. Hide in the bushes."

"Yes, that is true. I am afraid of them, but I will not pay what they ask. I do not pay for protection I do not need."

"Do you know the names of the men who threatened you?"

"No."

Ruben finished hammering the nails in the shoe and dropped Ginger's hoof. He spit the extra nails back into the keg and set his hammer down. He untied the halter rope and walked Ginger around in a small circle, observing how the horse walked.

"The shoe, it fits," he said to Brad.

Brad gave him a five-dollar gold piece. Ruben looked at it and smiled.

"Enough?" Brad said.

"I am rich."

They both laughed.

"So long, Ruben," Brad said. "*Ten cuidado.* Be careful."

"Ah, you speak the tongue. I will be careful."

Brad walked Ginger out of the blacksmith shop and down the street to the livery. There he saddled up and tied on his bedroll, slung his saddlebags behind the saddle, and after he climbed up, stuck his Winchester in its scabbard.

"All set?" Ethan said as he looked up at Brad.

"See you in a day or two," Brad said, and rode out into the sunlight. He looked up at the sky and marked the time of day by the sun's position. He rode out of town at a fast trot, anxious to get home.

He did not see the two riders who came down the street behind him. They headed for the livery stables, but stopped when they saw Brad ride away.

"That's him," Cole said.

"Who?" Tom asked.

"That's the damned Sidewinder, Tom."

"Damned if it ain't."

"That's fifty dollars riding yonder."

"Hell, he's gone already," Tom said. "We

missed our chance."

"We can foller the bastard."

"Yeah, we can do that. On empty stomachs. I'm hungry."

"Stay here and get you some grub, then. I'm goin' to go after him."

"Not without me, you ain't. Do we split the fifty?"

Cole gave it some thought.

"Yeah, sure. Come on."

The two men rode past the livery at a quick trot to the end of the street where they had seen their quarry turn toward the mountains.

They turned and looked down a road that was empty except for a pair of mangy dogs and a Mexican carrying a load of firewood tied with string on his back.

"Where in hell did he go?" Tom asked as they slowed their horses and rode down the street to its end, a pistol shot from the corner.

"Into the mountains, most likely. Look for his tracks."

Tom studied the ground.

"I see 'em," he said. "Real fresh. Them are the onliest ones can be the Sidewinder's."

"Keep your eyes peeled, Tom. We'll catch up to the bastard and put his lights out."

"We're supposed to be makin' calls on them Mexes what Finch told us to see."

"Hell, this shouldn't take more'n a half hour."

"Easiest fifty we'll ever make," Tom said.

They followed the tracks up a road that wound through the foothills. It was well rutted and showed signs of travel, but the fresh horse tracks were plain to see.

Tom's stomach growled, and he could feel his hunger gnawing away at him. But his mind was on the Sidewinder and half of that fifty dollars they would collect when they brought his body back to town.

Cole kept looking ahead, but the road was empty. After a few moments it disappeared among the hills. But he knew it would go on, and somewhere ahead of them was the Sidewinder, ripe for a shot in the back whenever they spotted him.

It would, he thought, be an easy kill.

Seventeen

Percy Willits, a cadaverous string bean of a man with a balding head that sprouted only a few bristly gray hairs, set the push broom in an empty cell. He wiped his bony hands on the faded blue bib of his patched overalls and looked in on Barney Jenkins, the jail's only prisoner.

Barney Jenkins was sprawled on a cot, his face turned to the wall. His hat lay under his bunk, a lifeless clump of brown felt that was stained with yellow and red condiments, blood and vomit. He wore a checkered shirt and rumpled trousers braced by dark blue suspenders. His work boots were scarred and torn, the heavy soles fairly new but caked with dried mud.

"You awake, Barney?" Willits called into the small cell with its twin bunks and a slop jar, a rusty drain hole in the center.

"Harrumph," Barney responded.

"Wanta play some cards?"

Barney turned over and blinked lashes over bloodshot eyes, eyes that looked boiled in beet juice, rheumy, with amber-stained whites.

He sat up and there was desiccated vomit on the front of his shirt.

"Naw, Percy. Not now. My head feels like it's full of hammerheads all jostlin' around on kettledrums."

"You was in better shape last night when Wally brung you in from the Lazy Dog Saloon."

"That where I was?"

"Yeah. Fightin' over a glitter gal old enough to be your ma."

"Suzie? Hell, she's only about twenty-five."

"Yeah, Suzie. She's forty if she's a day, and so ugly she gives me a hard-off."

"I like Suzie," Barney said with a tongue thickened by alcohol on a two-day drunk.

The two men were interrupted by the sound of the door opening in the sheriff's office out front.

"I better go see who that is," Percy said.

"Yeah."

"Want any grub?"

"Got any whiskey, Percy?"

Percy laughed and walked through the large room with its three jail cells and into the front office, which was the sheriff's. He locked the door behind him with a key on a large ring attached to his Sam Browne belt.

Alonzo Jigger put his hat on a standing rack and walked to the desk. He sat down behind it. Wally followed him in, keeping his hat on, and went to a smaller desk that was against the wall. His desk was stacked high with dodgers, some of which had turned brownish yellow from age. There was a box of thumbtacks, a tin ashtray full of cigarette butts and ashes, and an open package of Piedmont cigarettes.

"Who're you?" Percy asked, his voice a deep drone from his emaciated throat.

"I'm Jig, the new sheriff."

"Sheriff, this here is Percy Willits, your jailer. Percy, this is our new sheriff, Alonzo Jigger."

"You can call me Jig, Percy. You the only jailer?"

"No, sir, but Zeke Hunsacker's down with the croup. I been bunkin' in an empty cell the past three days."

"Well, you ain't goin' home today, Percy," Jigger said. "You et breakfast?"

"No, sir, I ain't. Rosie from the Oro Café generally brings lunch for me and my prisoners. I ain't usually here for breakfast. Zeke works from midnight to ten in the morning when he's not puny."

"Well, Percy, I want you to fetch me your prisoner. Wally says he brought in a drunk last night."

"You ain't takin' him afore the judge so's he'll get fined?"

"No, not today. You bring in your prisoner and then I want you to fetch me a notary public. There should be one somewhere around here."

"Yes, sir, they's a notary office over by the courthouse."

"Fine. Have him come over right away."

"You want me to put handcuffs on Barney? He ain't dangerous, just hungover."

"No, just bring him in here and set him in a chair by my desk."

"Yes, sir," Percy said and turned to unlock the door to the jail.

"Percy, can you read and write?" Jigger asked the jailer.

"Yes, sir. I had schoolin'."

"Good. Now fetch the prisoner."

Percy unlocked the door to the jail and went inside. Jigger looked through the desk drawers and pulled out a blank sheet of paper. He placed it on the desk and reached for the inkwell. He plucked a pen from a small wooden box and examined the tip of the quill. He grunted in satisfaction.

"What are you going to do, Sheriff?" Wally asked.

Flies buzzed in the room, flitting from window to window and down to Wally, who flicked them away with a wave of his hand. One landed on Jigger's desk and his hand shot to it. As it rose to fly away, he grabbed it in his left hand, closed his fist, and crushed the fly to a gob of guts and blood, its wings twisted into geometric angles like the broken wings of a bird. He wiped the palm of his hand on his trousers.

"You'll see soon enough, Wally," Jigger said.

Wally's mouth was still sagging open in amazement at the speed of Jigger's hand.

They heard a jingle of keys in the next room and the metallic sound of a lock being opened. Then the rattle of a cell door and the screech of iron as the door slid open.

Muffled voices and footsteps seeped into the office before Percy and his prisoner appeared.

"What's your name?" Jigger asked the prisoner, who stood next to the desk swaying slightly as if he was off balance on a high wire.

"Barnaby Jenkins. Folks call me Barney."

"Sit down."

Barney sat down in a chair that faced the desk.

"Can you read and write?"

"When I ain't in my cups."

"Are you in your cups now?"

"Maybe slightly." Barney rubbed the stubble on his chin and stared at the sheriff, stared at his badge, at his unruly red hair.

"Here's a piece of paper and a pen. Ink's in the well. I want you to start writing."

Percy stood there until Jigger looked at him.

"The notary," Jigger said.

"Oh, yes, I forgot. I'll go get him."

Percy reached the door in four strides, opened it, and went out onto the street. He passed the window like a skeleton wearing clothes and disappeared.

"What do you want me to write?" Barney asked, dipping the tip of the pen into the inkwell.

"Write down what I tell you," Jigger said.

"My script ain't none too good."

"Write so I can read it."

"All right."

Jigger began dictating:

" 'I, Tom Ferguson, witnessed a murder yesterday, east of town. My friend Ned Crawford and I was,' er no, make that 'were'."

"I didn't get that far," Barney said.

Barney wrote a few more words on the paper, then held the pen suspended.

"Okay, I got to 'were.' "

Jigger continued: " 'Were hunting rabbits when this stranger come up and tried to rob us. Ned shot at him and missed. The stranger shot Ned and killed him dead. The stranger run off, but he said he was called the Sidewinder. I found out his real name is Brad Storm.' "

Barney finished writing.

"Got all that?" Jigger asked.

"Yeah, I reckon so."

"Now sign it down at the bottom."

"But I ain't —" Barney started to say.

"Barney, how would you like to get out of here? No jail time?"

"That would suit me just fine, sir."

"Then sign it 'Tom Ferguson.' Real big letters."

"But, I ain't —"

"You want to get out of jail, don't you?"

"Well, sure, but —"

"Just sign it like I told you. Then you can go home or back to the bar where you get your medicine."

Barney signed "Tom Ferguson" in large cursive letters near the bottom of the paper.

Jigger reached over and took the pen from

his hands.

"Now, get the hell out of here, and if you ever mention this to anyone, I'll kill you. Got that?"

"Yes, sir, I got that."

He got up from his chair and started toward the jail.

"Where you going?" Jigger asked.

"I left my hat under the bunk."

"Clear out. You can buy another hat."

Barney turned and walked out the front door of the office. He stopped at the window and looked in as if to satisfy himself that what he had seen and done had truly happened. Then he ambled away, scratching his bare head.

Jigger turned to Wally as he held the paper up flat in front of his mouth and blew the ink dry.

"Wally, when that notary gets here, you're goin' to be a witness to this here document."

"I am?"

"You sure as hell are."

"But —"

"No buts. After you sign your name as a witness, you're going to take this here piece of paper over to the courthouse and ask Judge Leffingwell to issue an arrest warrant for Brad Storm, alias the Sidewinder."

"Holy shit," Wally said.

Jigger brought another blank sheet of paper out of the drawer and began writing on it with the pen.

He wrote "WANTED" in large block letters. Underneath, he wrote, in slightly smaller letters, "For the murder of Ned Crawford." And underneath that, he printed the words "Brad Storm."

Then, in larger letters, he wrote "REWARD $200."

"There a printer in town, Wally?"

"They's one over next to the *Leadville Register,* Sam Owens. And he does printing for the paper."

"Good. I want you to have Sam print up about twenty-five dodgers, and I want you to give the paper this story."

"I don't know," Wally said.

"We're going to get this Sidewinder bastard, Wally."

"Is this legal?"

"It's a means to an end."

"Well, you're the sheriff. I guess you can do what you want so far as the law is concerned."

"You're damned right I can."

Jigger caught another fly in midair and pinched it to goo between his thumb and forefinger.

His right hand was a blur of speed, Wally noticed. And the fly had appeared out of nowhere.

A man like Jigger, Wally thought, could probably outdraw any man alive. With a hand that fast, and an eye that good, no man would stand a chance against him in a gunfight.

Jigger wiped his fingers on the side of his boot, near the sole.

As he waited for Percy and the notary to arrive, Wally felt the first small temblers of fear in his stomach. He realized that he was in the same room with a very dangerous man, a man who would stop at nothing to achieve his ends.

If Jigger even suspected that he was helping Pete Farnsworth and Brad Storm in their investigation, Jigger would blow his brains out.

And never blink an eye.

Eighteen

Since his run-in with the rustlers, Brad never took the same road out of town when he meant to return to his modest ranch. Nor did he travel the same trail each time. The mountains around Leadville were criss-crossed with roads, trails, and footpaths. Some of the roads were dead ends. Others wandered into each other like the designs of a madman's maze.

But now he knew that someone was following him as he rode out of town. He didn't know who it was, but he had caught a glimpse of two men when he turned the corner. Two men who had made the mistake of riding down a street where riders seldom rode, a street with no stores, no warehouses, no public buildings with any access to them.

It was a street that was more like an alleyway than a thoroughfare.

Yet two men had taken that same street. He knew they were behind him. He didn't have to look back to see them.

The road he took out of town was more than a stone's throw from the Arkansas River and it was muddy and clean of wagon or hoof tracks. There were puddles in the ditches where dynamite had been placed to blow a road into the mountains long before he had come to what had once been called Oro City.

Brad reached back and pulled his canteen from one saddlebag and hung it from his saddle horn. Then he found the food Felicity had made for him in the other bag, beef sandwiches wrapped in paper and oilcloth. He stuck the sandwich inside his shirt with the intent of eating it when he had the chance.

He knew this country. He hoped the two men who followed him did not.

He left the muddy road when it made a bend, angling off to the left toward a creek that drained into the Arkansas River. The creek would conceal his tracks and allow him to circle his pursuers and wait for them in a more favorable location.

Brad's father had told him once, when Brad intended to go out West from Missouri, that he would find his way if he followed the rivers and the streams.

"There is where you will find game to

hunt and untouched land," his father had said. "The mountain men and the Indians thought of these rivers as great highways, and it has proven so since this country began settling west of the colonies."

Indeed, Brad's father had been right, and Brad had found his ranch by following the Arkansas and then the creeks that led him deeper into the mountains. Game trails, sheep trails, and old Indian trails provided him with a living road map of the country he had settled in and come to love.

White-barked aspen lined the creek, their green leaves all aflutter in the afternoon breeze. They looked like stately Greek columns decorated with laurel garlands, regal and beautiful in the dazzling sunlight that sprayed through them like a golden mist.

He rode into the grove of aspens, the soil soft and yielding beneath Ginger's feet, spongy along the bank of the creek. He stopped and looked down at his tracks. They were plain to see, and he smiled in satisfaction. Then he stepped Ginger into the creek and rode upstream for a quarter of a mile. He and Ginger climbed out of the creek at a bend where the water was shallow and he began to circle, heading back on a wide loop to where they had entered the water.

He rode to a place in the pines and spruce trees where he could see that same stretch of creek. There he concealed himself behind a large juniper tree and waited.

Brad heard their voices before he spotted them.

"Where in hell is he goin'?" one of the men asked.

"Damned if I know, Cole. Maybe his ranch is somewheres hereabouts."

Brad recognized the voice of the second man. It was the man he had disarmed at the guardhouse and sent down to the smelter with his message.

"Hell of a place for a ranch. Too many trees, not enough grass."

"Well, you never know," Tom Ferguson said, his voice drifting through the trees to Brad's ears. Brad slipped the set of rattles from inside his shirt and held them in his closed hand. The men were close, no more than fifty yards away, but he could not yet see them.

The creek burbled and sang as it coursed its way down to the Arkansas, a soft liquid sound like water pouring from a bottle into an oaken bucket.

"Hear that?" Cole said.

"Probably a crick up ahead," Ferguson said, a trace of annoyance in his voice.

"Shit," Cole said, and the two men rode into view, a little more than thirty yards from where Brad sat his horse, waiting.

Tom and Cole rode closer. They were wary now, and the two men drifted slightly apart. Brad recognized Cole as the man he had met on the road from the smelter, the one who had mistaken him for Alonzo Jigger. He smiled, and a brief thought flitted through his mind.

Two old friends, he thought.

The pair stopped at the creek where Ginger's tracks disappeared after the gelding had stepped into the creek.

"Damn," Tom said. "He knows we're trackin' him. Rode right into the damned crick."

"Maybe he just crossed it," Cole said. "Let's ride acrost it and see."

The two men rode across the creek, their horses splashing water with flashing hooves, the sounds slicing the air like silver knives. Splash, splash, splash, and they were across, once again on dry ground. The two men rode up and down that side of the creek, both leaning over and staring at the ground.

"See any tracks down your way, Tom?" Cole said.

"Nary."

"Ain't none here, neither. Damn."

"We could straddle both sides of the creek and ride up it. He's got to come out somewhere."

"Yeah, we can do that. You ride over to the other side and look real hard."

Brad shook the rattles before Tom could answer.

The rattles made a clacking sound like a thousand loose teeth shaking together and sent shivers up the spines of the two men at the creek.

"What's that?" Cole said.

"Rattlesnake," Tom said. "Unless . . ."

Brad shook the rattles again.

"Unless what?"

"Unless it's Sidewinder."

Brad shook the rattles once again, then slipped them back down his shirt. He rode out from behind the juniper just as Tom's hand slapped at the pistol on his hip.

He rode up on Cole and Tom, his pistol drawn.

"It's him," Tom said, and his right hand floated up from the butt of his holstered pistol.

"Damned if it ain't," Cole said, twisting in the saddle so that he could see Brad.

"You men hold real steady," Brad said as he rode up on them.

"You ain't goin' to shoot us in cold blood,

are you, mister?" Tom said.

"I just might."

"Hell, we ain't doin' you no harm," Cole said.

"A little ways off your range, aren't you?" Brad asked them.

"Just takin' a little ride is all," Cole said, a band of sweat ringing his neck just above his bandanna.

"We don't mean no harm," Tom said, sweat trickling down from his hairline in glistening rivulets like sweet cider.

"Take off your gun belts," Brad ordered. "Real slow, and keep both hands where I can see them."

"Shit," Cole said.

Brad poked the pistol at him and thumbed back the hammer.

The mechanism made a loud click, and blood drained from Cole's face.

Shadows of aspen leaves shifted on the ground, like hand shadows on a cave wall. They seemed to breathe in the silence that followed that ominous click of the hammer on Brad's pistol as the sear engaged inside the intricate mechanism of the lock. It sounded, Cole thought, like the single click of a giant clock, a clock that a man heard only at the last moment before his death.

"Wha-what you want to do this for, Side-

winder?" Tom asked. "We ain't done you no wrong."

"Unbuckle your gun belt, Tom."

Brad swung the pistol barrel to take aim on Ferguson's chest, that spot where the beating heart throbbed inside his chest, just under the fragile ribs that housed the delicate balloons of his lungs. Ferguson's left hand dropped to his buckle and he pulled on it to release the tongue. He dropped his other hand and tugged on the leather, springing the tongue out of the first hole.

Brad swung the pistol toward Cole again.

"Get to it," he said, and Cole began unbuckling his belt, sweat sheening his face as if a hose had been turned on inside his skull and was pushing moisture through the pores of his skin.

The leather of their gun belts creaked as tensions relaxed and the weight of the bullets acted like some kind of gravity hidden in cowhide. Both men held up their rigs with one hand as if to show Brad that they had complied and he no longer needed to threaten them with violence and death.

"Now drop them," Brad said. "Straight down on the ground."

The men opened their hands and their pistols, holsters, and ammunition belts fell like sash weights, the belts curling into snakelike creatures for just a second before they hit the soft ground with twin thuds.

"Now, Tom, you ease that rifle from its scabbard and toss it into the creek."

Brad's hand moved, and the pistol snout moved to stop on a direct line to the center of Tom's chest.

Tom jerked the rifle free and pushed its butt upward and outward. The gun hit the bank, toppled over, and the barrel splashed into the water.

"Now, you do the same with your rifle," Brad said, nodding toward Cole.

When Cole's rifle whacked off a tree some yards away, making a sound like a wooden mallet smacking into a sawhorse, both men winced and held their hands up over their heads as if surrendering would keep them both from dying now that they were unarmed.

"Step down and get at those saddles," Brad said. "One at a time, and make sure neither of you twitches or tries to run."

"You takin' our saddles?" Tom asked.

"Just do it. Strip your horses and let your saddles and all your stuff fall to the ground."

Tom finished pulling cinches and set his saddle down on its side beneath his horse's belly. Then Cole loosened his cinches and pulled his saddle from his horse's back.

"Jesus," Cole said.

"Now, both of you sit down and take off your boots. Hurry up. You're burning daylight."

Both men sat down and removed their boots. Anger contorted Cole's face as he tugged on the heel of one boot, then the other.

"Socks, too," Brad said.

"Christ," Cole said.

Brad gave him a sharp look. "Blasphemy's not helping your case, Cole."

Cole's lips moved as he mouthed a silent word that he dared not utter aloud.

"Now, both of you stand up and take off your clothes, hats and all."

"Now, that's far enough," Cole said.

"Mister, you don't know how far is far," Brad said. "Get to it. I can run out of patience faster than you can say another curse word."

The two men tossed their hats on the ground, unbuttoned their shirts, and slid out of their trousers.

They stood there, both of them naked, shivering in the chill breeze that flowed from the snowcapped mountains.

"You look like a couple of plucked chickens," Brad said, without any trace of humor in his voice.

"You bastard," Cole said, covering his privates with both hands like some modest maiden.

"You know the way back to town?" Brad asked.

Both men nodded.

"Then climb up on your horses and ride across that creek and head for town."

"My wallet's in my trousers," Tom said.

"Yeah, we ain't got no money, ner nothin'," Cole said.

"You can ask Earl Fincher for an advance on your pay," Brad said, moving his pistol again from one man to the other.

"What about our clothes and saddles and such?" Ferguson asked.

"When you get a ways toward town, you can look back up here and probably see the smoke."

"You goin' to burn our goods?" Cole asked.

"To a crisp," Brad said. "Now move."

Both men grabbed the reins and leaped up onto their horses' backs. They slithered and wriggled their bodies until they could slide into position astraddle their mounts.

"We'll get you for this, Sidewinder," Cole said as he turned his horse toward the creek.

"Yeah," Tom said, following in Cole's wake.

The two horses sloshed across the creek. Neither man looked back until they were both well out of sight.

When they did look back, they saw two thin columns of smoke rising into the sky.

"Not only did we lose our guns and saddles," Tom said, "but fifty bucks to boot."

"Aw, shut up, Tom. Just think about what Finch is goin' to say when we ride up to the hotel buck naked."

"Naked as jaybirds," Tom said, and shivered in the breeze, a bonewhite mannequin stripped of all pride and dignity, dreading the stares they would get when they rode into Leadville with the sun still up and no place to hide.

NINETEEN

Pete watched the ebb and flow of people, carts, horseback riders, women and men, cats, dogs, and pigs in front of the bank on Harrison Street. The ornate granite façade of the bank building with its perpendicular sculpture scrolls reminded him of Denver's California Street and the store where he had worked when he first met Harry Pendergast.

He had been working as a store clerk for the Denver Dry Goods Company on California Street in Denver. He began to notice not only shoplifters but other clerks who were stealing from the company, shortchanging some customers, pocketing money instead of putting it into the cash register. The store had hired Harry Pendergast to observe the pilferers and the dishonest clerks. Harry noticed that Pete was writing names and other observations down in a little notebook and approached him one day after work. The two went to a Larimer Street bar, and Pete showed Harry his notebook. Pendergast was able to catch the employees who were stealing from the company and round up the members of the shoplifting ring. He then offered Pete a job and trained him in the art of surveillance, undercover work, and a host of other detective skills.

Pete liked the work, but he was beginning to loathe the façade of the Leadville Bank & Trust. He particularly hated the word "Trust" in the title, since he was almost certain that someone in the bank was in cahoots with Fincher and his gang, the so-called Golden Council.

Paco kept bringing him coffee while Pete checked his pocket watch periodically, his gaze scanning the other buildings on the block, the Silver Slipper Saloon on the corner, and the notary public office, into which he had seen the jailer Percy Willits go and then reappear with Horace Kilbride, who later returned to the office alone. He made note of that and vowed to check with Wally or Percy later to find out why there was need of a notary at the Leadville jail. He suspected that Sheriff Jigger had sent Percy to fetch Horace. Then there was a pawn shop next to the notary's office, with pocket watches, musical instruments, jewelry, and other surrendered items in the window.

He also noted the front of the Oro City Land Office, which had not yet changed its name, right next to the Jefferson Assay Office and a small store that sold musical instruments, with guitars, trumpets, violins, and clarinets hanging in its windows, a full set of drums and cymbals taking center stage beneath the dangling instruments. This was the Harrison Music Company. The bank took up the rest of the block between Third and Fourth streets.

Around three fifteen, Pete saw the sulky pull up in front of the bank, and moments later, he observed Adolphus Wolfe, the bank owner, emerge and climb into the two-wheeled vehicle with its flamboyant red awning. He carried two heavy satchels, one in each hand, and he puffed from exertion as he took his seat. His face was florid and wet with a sudden sweat. He wiped his brow and face with a pale rose handkerchief he took from his back pocket. The driver turned the sulky in the middle of the street and drove it toward Fourth Street, where it turned the corner toward the fancy residential district and disappeared.

Pete watched the sun crawl along the

buildings for another few minutes. Shadows flowed into dark pools in between buildings and grew long hair that spread across a wet street that had turned to dust under the feet of traffic. It looked as if a sculptor was at work with subtle tools, shaping and reshaping Harrison Street without harming its basic structure or contours.

He watched a butterfly flit to a nearby table and alight in a sun-drenched corner. It flexed its yellow wings as if they were an extension of its lungs. The butterfly, he thought, was a symbol of reincarnation, of previous lives lived in other forms. He wondered if all humans had once been something else and were now in the last stages of a complex life cycle, the good, the bad, and the profane, all breathing the same air as that lone yellow-winged butterfly warming itself in the afternoon sunlight.

Pete gestured to his waiter, Paco, who came over.

"More coffee?" Paco said.

"No. See that woman just coming out of the bank?"

Paco looked across the street.

"I see her."

"Know her name?"

"Yes, that is Miss Andrews. She works at the bank."

"What's her given name?"

"I think they call her Betty. I believe her name is Elizabeth. She is a nice lady."

"Can you walk over and tell her to come here?"

"I don't know," Paco said.

"You know her."

"Yes, I know her. She comes here for lunch sometimes."

"Tell her a gentleman wants to talk to her. There's a silver dollar in my pocket for you if you'll do this."

"I will do it," Paco said. He slipped the towel from his arm and placed it on an empty chair at Pete's table. Then he scurried across the street as Betty Andrews was coming down the walk in her yellow cotton dress with a white piqué collar encircling her neck like a white sugar wafer, a blue belt around her waist. She carried a small doeskin purse and wore sensible low-heeled black shoes that showed off her delicate ankles.

He saw Paco speak to her and saw her look across the street at him. He raised a hand and beckoned to her. He saw her shake her head and then saw that Paco was still talking to her. She looked at him again and he smiled, lifted both arms at acute angles with his palms open to show that he meant her no harm. Then she and Paco began to walk toward him, avoiding a two-wheeled cart pulled by a gray burro that resembled a large mouse.

Paco led her to the table and picked up his towel. He stood facing Pete, his eyebrows raised, his brown eyes twinkling.

"Won't you sit down, Miss Andrews?" Pete said. "My name is Pete Farnsworth. Paco will bring you anything you like, a drink perhaps, or a sweet-cake if you wish."

She looked up at Paco, who had turned to face her like an obedient servant at attention.

"I'd like a cup of tea," she said in a voice that quavered with uncertainty, yet carried a hint of efficiency and intelligence. Her face was pear shaped, her lips faintly rouged, as were her smooth cheeks. She wore no mascara, and her eyes were as blue as an ocean on a calm day.

Paco nodded and scurried away.

Pete introduced himself and showed her his badge in its small leather wallet.

"Why ever would you wish to speak with me, Mr. Farnsworth?" she said, a coolness in her manner as well as a certain detachment. She placed her purse in her lap and folded her hands over it like a prim maiden at her first job interview.

"Two men, whom I believe were involved in robbery and murder, came into your bank this morning. They were carrying four burlap bags. Heavy bags. Do you recall them entering the bank?"

"Why, if I did, Mr. Farnsworth, that would be no business of mine, I assure you."

"But you saw them?"

"I may have."

The butterfly with the delicate yellow wings lifted off the table and flapped away like some scrap of old paper tossed by a vagrant breeze. Pete saw it lift off out of the corner of his eye and felt a brief surge of sadness, as if he had lost something important.

"They would be easy to spot, Miss Andrews. These were rough men, and they were lugging several bars of silver."

Betty Andrews gasped, either at the mention of silver or the fact that Pete knew what was in those burlap bags.

"I do not know what was in those bags. I directed them to Mr. Gorman, who opened the private vault for them. I believe they own a safe-deposit box in our bank."

Paco showed up with a small pot of tea, a cup and saucer. He set them in front of Betty and poured her cup half full. The steam and the aroma of Chinese orange pekoe drifted to Pete's nostrils. It was a pleasant smell. Paco deposited a slice of lemon in the saucer and laid a spoon upon a fresh napkin he spread next to her arm.

"Thank you, Paco," Pete said, dismissing him with his words.

"They really should serve the lemon slice with a fork instead of a spoon," she said. "With the fork, you can squeeze the lemon juice into the tea and the seeds won't fall in. But I never put lemon in my tea."

"There's a sugar bowl there," he said.

The white porcelain bowl was covered, and a tiny spoon handle jutted through the opening.

"I do not use sugar," she said, that prim look of propriety on her face.

"Neither do I. In my coffee, I mean."

"Either condiment dilutes the medicinal value of the tea," she said.

"Oh, come off it, Betty," he said with an abruptness that startled her. "You saw those men, and you know what they were putting in that safe-deposit box. Isn't that true?"

"I don't believe I care for your manner, Mr. Farnsworth."

"If you are concealing a crime, I can go to the sheriff and swear out a warrant for your arrest. I can also go before Judge Leffingwell and obtain a warrant to search that safe-deposit box."

"You wouldn't," she said, without a trace of conviction in her voice.

"Like hell I wouldn't. Now, I want to know what happened to those silver bars after those two men left the bank. Did anyone go into that safe-deposit box and remove them?"

Betty lifted the cup to her lips and drank to avoid answering Pete's question. The tea burned her tongue, and she reared back from the unexpected shock. Her purse slipped off her lap and fell to the flagstone floor.

Pete leaned down and picked up her purse. He looked at her slim legs, the light tan stockings that could not hide her graceful limbs.

He set the purse on the table in front of him, enclosed it between his arms and hands.

"My purse, if you please," she said, returning to her former prim position.

"Not until you answer my question. I saw Adolphus Wolfe leave the bank with two very heavy leather satchels. He could hardly lift them into his sulky. I'll bet you a month's salary those bags were weighted down with silver bars. Stolen sliver bars. Bars now bearing the intaglio of the Golden Council with the head of a wolf under the letters 'GC.' "

A look of shock came over Betty's face, and the rouge seemed to grow pale on her cheeks.

"Better take another jolt of that tea, Miss Andrews," he said.

Betty raised the cup to her lips. She drained it and set her empty cup down in the saucer. Pete poured the cup full, nearly to the brim.

"I can ask Paco to bring you something stronger," he said. "If you need it."

"You'll give me back my purse if I tell you what you want to know?"

"Sure. I'd look funny walking back to the Clarendon with your purse in my hand."

A little nervous laugh rippled from Betty's throat.

"Mr. Wolfe asked me to get him two large satchels out of the closet in his office. I did that. He carried them to the safe-deposit vault, and when he returned to his office, they were full, I suppose. Because they were heavy. He opened one after he sat down at his desk. He took out a silver bar and held it up to the window so the light would make it shine. He looked at the bar for a long time, then put it back in the satchel. When he left, he carried the satchels with him, although I offered to help."

"Is that the first time you've ever seen him with silver bars?" Pete asked.

"No. It is the same each time, although mostly it's money the men bring in to the bank. He counts the money and calls in Mr. Wheatley or Mr. Gorman. The money goes into a special account."

"The Golden Council?"

"No, I think it's a special account. I don't know the name. It might be only a number."

"You did fine, Miss Andrews."

"You won't tell anyone about this, will you?"

"It's just between you and me."

"And you won't take me to court or have me arrested?"

"Nope. I'll buy you supper if you like."

She sipped her tea and looked over the rim at Pete.

"Maybe," she said. "Not tonight, though. I live with my mother, and she's old and ailing. If you let me know a day or so ahead of time, I might be able to arrange for a friend to watch her while I go out."

It was then that they both heard strange sounds coming from down the street. They both turned to look. Paco, nearby at another table, stopped in midstride and stared.

People in the Chez Paris began to laugh and point.

"There are the two men who brought the silver bars to your bank, Miss Andrews," Pete said.

Betty blushed as Cole and Tom rode past the restaurant, heading for the river.

"Well, I never . . ." Betty gasped. She bowed her head in shame.

"Naked as a couple of newborn babes," Pete said. "They must have run into my friend, Brad Storm."

Betty Andrews did not have the least idea what Mr. Farnsworth was talking about.

Twenty

The cow lumbered away from the herd. Its pace was slow and deliberate as it headed for the pines across one of the creeks. It was very fat, its sides bulged out to massive proportions. It breathed with great difficulty and its brown eyes were moist and large with panic. Its white face contrasted starkly with its curly brown hide. Its small horns swung from side to side in slow motion, as it waded the creek, swollen from the rains of the night before, running swift so that the cow made slow progress through the flowing blue-black waters, whitecaps forming above its ankles, the foam boiling like soapy water in a heated kettle.

"She goes to drop her calf," Carlos said to Julio. He spoke in rapid Spanish. "Do I turn her back?"

Julio shook his head.

"No. She will not go far. The calf wants to get out. The cow picked that place a week ago. There is a little place of grass inside those pines. That is her *querencia.*"

Carlos Renaldo nodded. He knew what *querencia* was from the bullfights he had watched as a boy in his native town of Jalisco, in Mexico. That was the place the bull always went to when it was tiring and knew that it was going to die. That was the bull's place of preference in the ring when the crowd was roaring and cheering and the people were waving their arms. The torero had spiked its body with banderillas and was standing still, with cape and sword, waiting for the bull to lower its head so that he could charge in and plunge the sword between its shoulder blades. It was death in the afternoon for the bull, and the last thing it would see was the red silk cape and the oncoming *traje de luces,* the brilliant suit of lights the matador wore. The bull would never see the sword, for it was hidden behind the cape, but it would snort blood and fall to its knees as the matador danced by and the crowd cheered and waved its arms in a triumph that was not theirs.

"Will we watch her give light?" Carlos said.

"Yes, when she lies down, we will cross the creek."

"The cow is very big."

"The calf will be big and strong."
"That will be the first."
"It is the season," Julio said.
"And for your woman, as well, no?"
"Pilar is getting close, yes. She will give light very soon."
"Ah, a son."
"Maybe," Julio said, and the two men saw the cow reach the opposite bank, dripping water from its legs and belly as it entered the copse of pines and began to walk in a circle, trampling down the grass to make its bed.
Julio looked up at the sky and to the west, where the red sun was standing over the mountains. Fresh snow blanketed the entire range, and it shone like some gigantic alabaster fortress, blinding to gaze at, magnificent with all that whiteness. The snow glinted all the colors of the rainbow, flashing dots in a radiant spectrum that dazzled and danced across the vast expanse of fields.
"The sun will go down soon," Julio said.
"And there will be much cold this night."
"Let us see how soon the cow gives light to the calf."
They waited, their horses pawing the ground, tossing their heads, their tails switching at deerflies, their whickers of

impatience rumbling in their long throats. Julio's horse, Chato, was a pinto, while Carlos rode a bob-tailed dun named Tico.

The cow moaned, and its body began to heave with contractions. She twisted on the mashed-down bed of grass and groaned in the throes of birthing. Her eyes glassed over with pain as a tiny head appeared, wrapped in a gossamer film, its pink snout pushing outward.

"It comes," Carlos said.

"Yes, it pushes into the world and does not yet see it."

The calf emerged, its forelegs pulling free of the cow's womb, its eyes closed, its face still wrapped in filmy white that was not yet parting and sliding away from its snout. The cow spilled the calf out, and it lay quiet, exhausted, as the yellow oval of afterbirth spewed out like the yolk of a broken egg. The cow struggled to its feet and turned to its calf. It began to lick away the gauzy substance that enveloped the small creature, and nudged the calf's tiny belly with its nose, urging it to its feet.

"It lives," Carlos said.

The calf stood on wobbly legs, and its mother moved so that it could get to her udder. The calf lifted its head and poked her in the belly, sniffing out the milk, until it found a teat, slipped its mouth over the nipple, and began to nurse.

The sun slid lower in the sky, and its lower rim dipped behind the far peaks. The snowy mantle began to dim ever so slightly, and the shadows of the grazing cattle stretched across the field in long, dark silhouettes attached to their bodies and feet.

"Julio, come quick."

Both men heard the woman's voice calling across the field, thin and high with a note of anxiety.

"That is not Pilar," Carlos said.

"No, it is Felicity."

"You should go to her, then."

"Yes. You stay here and see that the calf does not wander into the creek and drown."

"For sure," Carlos said.

Julio turned his horse and headed for the house and buildings at the far end of the large pasture. He headed straight for Brad's house, where he could see a small figure standing outside waving her arms. He put Chato into a gallop, and the horse pulled its elongated shadow along behind it, the grasses rumpling the dark image so that it rippled like waves on a green sea.

"Julio, hurry," Felicity called, then turned and ran into her house.

Julio's stomach swarmed with fluttering

insects as a nameless fear gripped him. He wondered what was wrong. He had heard the urgency in Felicity's voice but saw no outward signs of trouble. There was no fire or smoke coming from the log house, the horses were already in the barn, and there was no sign of Pilar at his own house or anywhere near the house where Carlos bunked.

He crossed himself and dug rowels into Chato's flanks, lashing his rump on both sides with the trailing ends of his reins.

The mountains were devouring the sun, pulling it down into the maw of another world that waited for its golden rise thousands of miles away.

He reined up Chato a few yards from the door and swung out of the saddle, hitting the ground at a dead run. He saw a glow beyond the door as someone lit a lamp and yellow light flared against the shadows of the room. He stepped into a yellowish mist that blinded him for a moment.

"Julio, my Julio," gasped Pilar. She was lying on the divan, her hands splayed atop both sides of her swollen belly.

He ran to her and knelt down, caressed her face with his left hand. She was drenched in sweat.

"What passes?" he said in Spanish.

"I do not know," Pilar said. "It hurts much."

He felt a soft hand on his shoulder and turned to look up at Felicity, whose face was drawn, bone white with strain and worry.

"You must hitch up the wagon, Julio," Felicity said. "We must get Pilar to a hospital in Leadville."

"Does not the baby come?" he said.

"No. It is something else. Something I can't help her with. Hurry. We will put blankets and pillows in the wagon bed. She needs a doctor."

"Do you know a doctor?" he said as he rose to his feet.

"Yes, and he has an infirmary, like a small hospital, where he can —"

"Is she to die?"

"Not if we hurry."

"It is a long way to the town and the night is coming."

"We will take lanterns. Hurry, Julio, please hurry."

Pilar groaned in pain. Julio rushed outside and ran to the barn. He went inside and selected two horses to pull the wagon. He put them both into harness and led them outside, backed them up to the wagon, and attached the tongue between them. By the time he was finished, the sun had disappeared from the sky and there was only a glowing furnace, far away and cold, beyond the white mountains.

Venus appeared in a pale blue region, a lone sparkling diamond in a sea turning black on some eastern shore where the darkness had already arrived.

Julio pulled the horses and wagon to the front of the cabin and set the brake. Felicity met him at the door, a pile of blankets in her arms.

"I'll get more and some pillows," she said as Julio carried his load to the wagon.

Carlos wondered what Julio was doing. He could barely see the houses and thought he heard the creak of a wagon. But it was already getting dark and difficult to see. The cattle in the pasture were dim statues that did not seem to move, although he knew they still grazed.

The cow and her calf lay down, and he knew they would not try to cross the creek.

He turned his horse and then heard something that stiffened all the vertebrae in his spine. The crunch of a twig, the rustle of a leaf, the heavy breath of a large animal.

"Hello, Carlos."

Carlos whipped his head around and saw

the horseman loom up behind him. He reached for the rifle in his boot.

"It's me, Carlos, you blind bastard."

"Eh, Brad? That is you? *Dios mío,* I do not hear you."

Brad rode up alongside him.

Two rifles were lashed in his bedroll, and two pistol rigs hung from his saddle horn. He pointed to them.

"I brought you and Julio a couple extra rifles and a pair of pistols."

"Oh, you bought those for us?"

"I took them from men who do not deserve them."

"Did you shoot these men? Did you kill them?"

"Not yet," Brad said. "Where's Julio?"

Carlos told him what had happened, and showed him the dim shapes of the cow and calf.

"I think Julio has hitched up the wagon and has pulled it to your house."

"Let's get up there and find out what's going on."

"Do you think the new calf and its mother will be all right?"

"I think they both know what to do, Carlos. Come on."

It was full dark when Carlos and Brad rode up to the cabin.

The tailgate was down and the wagon bed was piled with spread blankets and pillows.

"Brad, you help Julio carry Pilar to the wagon," Felicity said. "We must get her to town where Doc Rankin can take a look at her."

He saw the anguish in Felicity's face as he swung down off his horse.

"Put those rifles and pistols somewhere, Carlos," Brad said as he followed Julio into the house.

They lifted Pilar from the divan and carried her gently out to the wagon. Felicity had climbed up, and she helped guide Pilar over the blankets. Both men climbed up and arranged Pilar on her makeshift bed.

"I'll get more blankets to put over her," Felicity said. She jumped down from the wagon and went inside the house.

She emerged carrying a food hamper and two more blankets and a heavy quilt.

"There are lanterns on the seat," she told Brad. "I'll drive the wagon. You follow us, Brad."

"Let's think this through," Brad said. He saw Carlos riding back from his bunkhouse. The outlaws' rifles and pistols were gone.

"Or maybe you can drive and Julio and I will tend to Pilar," Felicity said.

"It so happens that I need a man or two

in town to help me," Brad said. "So here's what we're going to do. Carlos will drive the wagon. I'll ride ahead to lead the way. You and Julio stay with Pilar."

"Oh, Brad," Felicity said. "I'm so glad you're finally here to help. I was at my wits' end."

"You did well," he said. Then, to Carlos, "Close the tailgate, tie your horse and Julio's to the back of the wagon. I see you strapped on one of those new pistols."

"To see how it would fit."

"Keep it on. You may have need of it."

"I am wearing my pistol," Julio said. "Always."

"Good," Brad said.

"Have you eaten, Brad?" Felicity asked. "I have food in the hamper."

"I ate," he said. He climbed into the saddle and rode up alongside the wagon as Carlos got into the driver's seat and picked up the reins.

"Brad," Felicity said, "is there something you're not telling me? What happened in town? Why didn't you come home last night?"

"Felicity, there's a lot I'm not telling you. This doesn't seem the time for that."

"But I want to know."

"You will," he said. "I promise."

He rode into the pasture as Carlos released the brake and the wagon rattled into a turn.

Venus sparkled in a vast ocean of stars that twinkled like cut diamonds on a dark velvet tapestry. They looked like the lights of distant towns millions of miles away, mirages that only appeared at certain times when most men's eyes were closed and could not see nor imagine them.

Brad saw them as they all rode out of the vast valley, and he drew comfort from them. They were his map to anyplace he wanted to go, and when the moon rose, there would be light and they would not need the lanterns that bonged and clanged in the wagon seat next to Carlos.

Brad felt right at home in the darkness of night. If it were up to him, he would ride and ride and never come to a town. Towns were the breeding grounds of greed and avarice, treachery and injustice, the places where men preyed on men and where corruption rose up with its ugly head and tried to swallow all that was good and decent, all that was precious and rare.

He was sorry that he had to take his little family into Leadville.

Even to save a life or two.

Twenty-One

The Carmody Hotel was among the oldest structures on Pine Street. Its pine logs had been patched with scraps of whipsawed lumber over the years. Yet it stood among even older buildings, shabbier ones, the earliest made of adobe bricks that had crumbled to dust and been replaced by ugly plugs of cement or stuffed with old rags and crumpled air-tights and mortared over with flimsy plaster that had to be replaced almost every cold spring.

The ride down Harrison Street to Pine and then to the Carmody seemed the longest in Cole Buskirk's life, with the humiliating laughter and the gawkers coming out of stores to gaze at the two naked riders. Even a reporter from the *Leadville Register* had run out from the newspaper office to mark their passing with hastily scribbled words in his notebook before rushing back into the office to write an account for the next edition. The editor called in a sketch artist to draw an illustration, and the compositors set up a chase and started laying type and furniture to record the event for posterity.

Earl Fincher and Lenny Carmichael both heard the commotion and came out on the boardwalk to see Cole and Tom ride up to the hotel's hitching rail.

"Boy, I've seen some sorry sights in my time," Fincher said, "but you two take the cake."

"What happened to your duds?" Carmichael said as the two men dismounted and walked to the hotel porch. An old man in the lobby looked out through the window, gasped, and ran to the bar for a drink, exclaiming, "They's wild men out there comin' to chop us all up and eat us!" He had already had a few drinks that same day, but his rheumy eyes, he insisted, did not lie.

"Finch, can you bring us a blanket or something?" Cole asked.

"You need duds," Lenny said, a rabid smile on his face.

"And we ain't got none," Fincher said.

The two men stood there shivering, their hands crossed in front of their privates. Finch puffed on a cheroot and gave them both a look of pure disgust. He reached into his pocket and pulled out that same fifty-dollar gold piece he had offered as a reward to anyone who killed the Sidewinder. He passed it to Carmichael.

"Lenny, run down to that dry goods store on Harrison and buy these men some duds. Cheapest you can get."

"What all?" Lenny asked.

"Pants, boots, hats, belts."

"We ain't got no guns," Ferguson whined.

"In due time, in due time," Fincher said. "Now follow me up to my room and have a drink of rotgut while you tell me why I shouldn't shoot both you boys dead for ridin' here nekkid as a pair of plucked chickens."

The aroma of the Arkansas River permeated Fincher's room on the second floor of the hotel. Room 208 was at the end of a dim hallway, and the window in Fincher's room was open and overlooked the river. Garbage swirled in its eddies, and the smell of rotted food, human fecal matter, urine, driftwood, and cow and horse dung seemed to cling to the worn-out furniture, the tired and shabby drapes, the threadbare carpet, and the Spartan bedding. There was but one table, a bed with a sagging mattress and faded covers, two rickety chairs, a bureau, and a wardrobe in the room. A chamber pot, reeking of soap, sat near the bed. Atop the bureau, there was a porcelain pitcher, two dirty glasses, and one of Fincher's battered tin cups, along with a bottle of whiskey in an unlabeled bottle. The bottle was three-quarters full.

"Sit down, boys, and spin your yarns," Fincher said. "I'll pour you a little whiskey to loosen your tongues."

"Well, we saw him, Finch," Cole said.

"It was him all right," Tom said.

Fincher poured whiskey into the glasses and handed them to Cole and Tom. Both men had chilblains on their arms from the fresh breeze ruffling the drapes and surging silently into the room.

Both men drank from their glasses and pulled their elbows close to their bodies as if to ward off the chill.

"Who?" Fincher said. He sat on the edge of the bed, and the wooden slats creaked under his weight. Dust puffed up from the bedspread, adding to the musty scent of the room.

"The Sidewinder," Cole said. "Saw him ridin' out of town, plain as day."

"You're sure it was him?" Fincher said.

"It was him all right," Ferguson said again. "Headed for the mountains all by his lonesome."

"And?" Fincher said.

"We follered him," Cole said. "Kept our distance so's he couldn't see us. He rode across the plain into the hills on an old road. We stayed back until we knew he couldn't see us. Road was still muddy and a mite damp, so's his tracks was plain to see."

"Tell me you put his lamp out, Cole," Fincher said, his voice laden with a sarcasm that grated like a metal spatula scraping grease off the bottom of an iron skillet.

"He got the jump on us up in the hills," Cole said.

"Hell, he was waitin' for us," Tom said. "Knowed we was follerin' him all the damned time."

"You dumb sonsabitches," Fincher said.

"He got the drop on us, Finch. No fault of our'n. We was real careful and quiet." Cole poured more whiskey into his mouth and gullet. "Can we close that winder, Finch? My balls are freezin' off."

"I ought to cut them off," Fincher said. But he walked to the window and pulled it down. He did not close it all the way, but left two inches of space between the pane and sill. He stood there, looking down at the river. A bittern pecked at a half-eaten apple. Crows hopped along the shore, cackling in throaty chatter as they fought over scraps dragged from the river. The sun painted quavering orange and red ribbons atop the flowing waters, silvered the rims of wavelets and ripples, pushed shadows back and forth, glistening one moment, subdued the next, as if the river were a serpent snaking over the earth, its scales rippling and undulating as it crawled, hissing, to the distant unseen sea.

"Hell, them hills and mountains is Sidewinder's country, not ours, Finch," Cole said.

Fincher walked back to the bed and sat next to a pillow, stretching his legs out over the coverlet. His boots made brown scars on the cotton surface, smears of caked dirt and horse manure.

"You should have shot him when he was crossing that plain."

"Too far away for a clean shot," Tom said. "Hell, I thought about it. We figgered we could get up close, brace him, and drop him from his dadgummed saddle."

"You got the brain of a pissant, Tom," Fincher said.

"I thought we might foller him to his ranch, you know, and find out where he lived and just wait for a clean shot." Cole finished the whiskey in his glass and held it out for a refill.

Fincher shook his head.

"No more whiskey for either of you. I'm waiting for the rest of the story. Seems like he not only got the drop on both of you, but made you strip naked, shuck your saddles and such. Took your damned rifles and pistols and sent you packin' back to town."

"I reckon that's what happened," Tom said.

"You both got shit for brains," Fincher said.

Both men hung their heads, sheepish expressions on their faces.

"It was downright humiliatin', Earl," Tom said.

"And now both you boys are the damned talk of the town. You got no guns, got no saddles, lost your hoods, and are absolutely worthless to me."

"When we get us some clothes, and if you'll advance us some cash, we can —"

Cole was interrupted by a knock on Fincher's door.

"Come in," Fincher said.

The door opened and Lenny Carmichael came in carrying a large bundle wrapped in brown paper. He dumped the bundle on the table and wiped his moustache with the back of his hand.

"I hope they fit," he said and sat down on

the opposite side of the bed. The bed slats groaned.

He pulled a handful of bills and some change from his pocket and laid them on the bed next to Fincher's leg. Fincher stared at the bills but made no move to pick them up or count the money.

Cole and Tom set down their empty glasses on the table. Cole unwrapped the clothes and held up a shirt.

"Looks right," he said.

Tom reached for the other shirt on top and stood up. Fincher turned away from them in disgust as they slid into new trousers and ran their belts through the loops, buckling them tight. They pulled on boots over bare feet.

Cole glared at Lenny.

"No damned socks, Carm?"

"Earl didn't say to get you no socks," Lenny said. "And don't call me 'Carm.' "

Earl and Tom walked back and forth in their new boots, the soles and the leather creaking from the newness and the stiffness.

Fincher looked at them again, the trace of a smirk on his face.

"I don't know what to do with you two," he said. "You're absolutely worthless to me at this point."

"What about the Mexes?" Cole said. "We

can still do our jobs. Maybe get us pistols real cheap at that pawn shop up on Harrison."

"I've already shelled out good money for them clothes," Finch said.

"Hell, we're good for it, Earl," Cole said. "You know that."

"Yeah," Fincher said and arose from the bed. He picked up the money and counted the bills. He put the coins in his pocket.

"There's enough left of that fifty for you both to get you a couple of two-dollar pistols at that pawn shop. You can carry them in your pockets or in your belt. You get forty-fives and we can give you ammunition. Right, Lenny?"

"Yeah, I got plenty in my saddlebags and on my gun belt."

"I'll see you boys back here at sundown and we'll go after them Mexes."

He handed the wadded up bills to Cole while Tom looked on, feeling cheated.

"Two-dollar pistols?" Tom said.

"That's all your sorry ass is worth," Fincher said. "Now get the hell out of here."

"We ain't got no saddles," Cole said, stuffing the bills in his pocket.

"You rode in bareback," Fincher said. "You can ride back to the smelter bareback."

Cole and Tom tried on their hats. Tom's

was a tad too large for a good fit and slid down over his eyebrows. Cole's was too small for his head. The men exchanged hats and began to crimp the crowns as a sign of ownership and personal distinction.

Fincher watched both men walk out of his room and close the door.

"They look like a pair of greenhorns," Carmichael said.

"Dumb pilgrims, you mean."

He walked over to the window and raised it back to its former position. He leaned out to mark the position of the sun over the mountains. The light slanted and gave a different texture to the river, gilding the small whitecaps, burning orange veins into its rippling fabric, pushing shadows under the far bank, and glinting off the satin feathers of the squawking, squabbling crows that hopped along the shore in sacerdotal splendor as if they owned the world.

Fincher walked to the bureau and opened the top drawer. He pulled out his gun belt and strapped it onto his waist.

"Too bad about that Sidewinder," Lenny said, rising from the bed.

"Well, if he's up in the mountains, we don't hardly have to worry about him, do we?"

"Not right now, I reckon."

"It'll be dark soon. We better saddle up and get to work. Once that sun falls behind the mountains, it'll get dark real fast."

As if echoing Fincher's words, the window darkened slightly and the golden rays no longer glazed the windowpane. The glass shimmered in the gathering dusk that softened the earth and gathered shadows into the river like clumps of dirty laundry floating downstream.

TWENTY-TWO

Esmerelda Sanchez put two more sticks of kindling into the firebox of her small woodstove. They would keep the tamale pie she had baked warm until Ruben came home for supper. She brushed her long black hair to a satin shine for the next fifteen minutes as she sat in front of a broken mirror on her dressing table. She had salvaged the fragment from a refuse dump down by the river, and it gave her much pleasure to be able to see her face, although part of the mirror was blackened from a fire and the rest of it was lightly smoked so that her reflection was slightly dimmed. She didn't mind that because it gave her a mysterious allure when she sat back and viewed her pretty oval face with the high Yaqui cheekbones, petite nose, and eyes dark as olive pits.

She turned her head one way, then the other, then leaned closer to the mirror to see if there were any blemishes on her face.

Her skin was as smooth as velvet and copper-toned. Ruben told her that she looked like an Aztec princess, and her heart always pounded faster when he talked that sweet way. Her lips were small but full and bore the faint trace of the same rouge she had rubbed into her slightly hollow cheeks. She smelled of jasmine, the fragrance her husband liked best, and it blended well with the scent of flowers that stood in the small modest vases she had placed in the front room, in the bedroom, and in the kitchen window. There were morning glories, petunias, and lilacs that she had grown in her yard.

The house was small, but she liked it because it did not take much time to clean. There was a front room with its three large windows, a bedroom, and a small kitchen. Ruben had built a small porch in front and a larger one in back where he sometimes worked on his iron sculptures that he sold at the small *abarrotes* store on the corner or at the open air *mercado* over by the river on weekends or special occasions. He had a forge and tongs, hammers, and a large kiln, almost like an *horno,* a dome-shaped oven, in the backyard, and a bellows he kept in the bedroom closet. He was a hard worker, and she admired the work he did at home because she knew it was art and took his mind off the labor of shoeing horses for a living.

Esmerelda finished brushing her hair and walked out to the backyard to breathe the fresh air and watch the sunset. Ruben never got home before dark, and she always looked out at the mountains to see how long it would be before he got home.

The sky to the west was filled with long purple clouds, their bottoms lined with shimmering gold leaf, their tops with blazing silver. Radiant light streamed from a fiery furnace behind the snow-mantled range, spreading heavenward in misty beams that made her think of the stained-glass windows in the little Catholic church in Tesquiapan.

She heard the birds of dusk announcing the night and saw the bats flitting like scraps of black crepe in the afterglow. There was the zinging of insects in her ear and the clatter of crickets in the grass that grew from green to gray in the fading light of day.

She went back into the house and walked through the front door to sit on the front porch and wait for Ruben. It was darker there, and she felt the loneliness of evening descend upon her like her mother's black shawl. She missed her mother, who had been dead for five years.

She heard Ruben coming down the street long before she saw him. There was the rumble of iron wheels and the clunking together of wagon springs, metal rods, cans, and strips of tin and copper he had salvaged from one place or another, and the clop of the horse's hooves as it pulled his cart.

She stood up when he loomed into view, like a knight returning from a crusade, and she could smell his manly sweat and the musty odor of the horse's hide. She smiled and felt her body tingle all over with pleasure as she ran into the street to throw her arms around him, have him clasp her tight and pepper her neck with soft kisses that made her shiver with delight.

"I can smell the food," he said.

"You should smell me, not the tamales, Ruben."

"Ah, you. I smell you all day long and my loins burn with desire for you."

She felt the heat of the blush that burst on her face like warm lotion, and she held his hand as they walked the horse to a shed at the side of the house, where Ruben kept feed and water and the two-wheeled cart he had built himself.

"You will unload the scrap metals tonight?" she asked.

"Not tonight, *querida.* In the morning. Go inside. I will unhitch Paquito and hobble him."

"I will set our plates on the table. I will light a lamp."

"Light a candle on the table. I have brought wine for us to drink with our supper."

She giggled as she ran away and into the house.

"And," he called after her, "I have brought gold for my princess."

When he came into the house, he washed his hands in the bowl she had placed on the sink board, and she handed him a towel. The bottle of wine was on the table. She had uncorked it and poured it into a glass cruet.

"You must let the red wine breathe before you drink it," she said. "That is what my father told me."

"Your father was a wise man, Merelda."

"Not as wise as you, my Ruben."

They ate and talked like young lovers dining in a fine restaurant. The food smelled good and tasted even better, he told her. Then he laid the five-dollar gold piece next to her plate.

"For you," he said.

"For me? Where did you get it?"

"I stole it from a *bandido,*" he said. "A cruel and very ugly bandit."

"Oh, you. You did not."

He told her about the man who had wanted his horse shoed and paid him five dollars for a task that took only a few minutes.

"He was a very nice man, but he asked me a lot of questions."

"What kind of questions?"

"He asked me if I paid the protection, if I bought the insurance. He asked about the Golden Council."

"What did you tell him?"

"I told him I would not pay such men for doing nothing."

"Good for you, Ruben. I am very proud of you."

She picked up the gold piece and put it inside her bodice, a coy look on her face.

"If you want it back, you will have to take all my clothes off," she said.

He laughed and reached across the table for her. She reared back, laughing, and stood up.

"Later," she said. "I will wash the plates. Will you smoke the pipe?"

"Not tonight. I am tired. I am shoeing the horses from the Panamint."

"Ah, the big horses."

"Yes, very big."

They both froze a moment later, she at the sideboard in the kitchen, he at the table, when they heard the sound of horses galloping down the street. The sound grew louder and louder.

"What is it, Ruben?" she said, her voice tight with fear, as if someone had a hand on her throat.

"I do not know. Stay where you are."

He walked into the front room as four men rode up, turned their horses into the yard.

Ruben backed away.

"Where is my pistol?" he husked.

"I-I think you put it on the shelf in the closet."

"Get it," he whispered. The whisper was loud. She felt the throb of her heartbeat as she ran into the bedroom.

"What is it?" she called from the other room.

Ruben saw the men as they dismounted.

They all wore yellow hoods, and when they had alighted, they drew their pistols.

He was powerless to stop them as they broke the latch on the front door and pushed their way in. He raised his arms to ward them off as they charged straight toward him.

One of them lifted his pistol and used it like a club to smash Ruben in the head.

"This is where you learn the value of insurance, Mex," one of the men said.

Then Ruben heard Esmerelda scream from the bedroom and his blood froze to ice in his veins. Lights danced behind his eyes and he felt his knees turn to jelly. His legs gave way, and he saw only the yellow hoods and the black eyeholes, the pink and obscene lips of wet mouths through the slit.

Then rough hands grabbed his arms and jerked him upright. He felt himself being dragged across the room.

Esmerelda came out of the bedroom, holding his pistol in her hand.

She screamed as the hooded men swarmed over her. One of them snatched Ruben's pistol from her hand.

Esmerelda kept screaming.

Ruben felt his heart being torn from his chest. He felt it being squeezed and the blood spurting from it like some diabolical fountain, drenching his brain, drowning his thoughts, and blowing through his eyes like an explosive somewhere inside his brain and deep in his soul.

Twenty-Three

Dr. Thaddeus Rankin lived in a small house next to his clinic and infirmary on Green Street in the northeast section of Leadville. He was awakened, near midnight, by one of his orderlies, Rufus O'Brien.

"What is it?" Thad Rankin asked as he sat up in bed. He rubbed his eyes and held a hand over them to shut out the yellow glare of the lantern in O'Brien's hand.

"Pregnant Mex woman at term. Baby seems to be blocked somewhere in the birth canal."

"Dammit, Rufus, they aren't Mexes. They're people of Mexican descent. Show a little courtesy."

"There's a white man and woman with 'em. I think you know the man."

"Who is he?"

"Brad Storm, he says."

"Tell them I'll be there momentarily, Rufus. Now get that damned light out of my eyes. I can dress in the dark."

O'Brien swung the lantern to one side and lowered it to a point just above his right knee.

"I've summoned Mrs. Brummage, Doctor. She should be at the infirmary by the time you arrive."

"Lord," Rankin exclaimed, "Mrs. Brummage? Excellent."

"Yes, sir. And there's one other thing I must bring to your attention."

"Damn, Rufus, what is it?"

"I've dispatched our ambulance to pick up some Mexes, I mean folks, who are badly beaten up. I believe the woman was raped and her husband soundly thumped. Their neighbor rode in an hour ago, and Billy Letterman drove the ambulance out to their residence."

"Lord," Rankin said again, "why in hell does everything happen at once?"

"It just does," Rufus said as Rankin waved him away from his bedside.

Rufus left the room. Dr. Rankin climbed out of bed in his long nightshirt and stripped it off over his head. He dressed in five minutes, grabbed his medical bag next to the door, and hurried to the infirmary. He saw the wagon outside the building with two saddled horses tied to the back and a pair in harness. The pale pile of blankets and pillows shone in the moonlight like rumpled shrouds covering gravestones.

He walked under the roofing over which hung the large sign RANKIN CLINIC & INFIRMARY. Under this legend, in smaller letters, was THADDEUS RANKIN, MD, CORONER.

He strode through the empty waiting room with its chairs and benches, lamps burning on small tables in two corners. He pushed open one of the double doors on leather hinges and stopped at a hall tree. He set his bag down and slipped a light tan coat over his white shirt. He picked up his bag and hurried past the five unoccupied beds to the last one, where he had heard the whispers and murmurs of those standing around the bed. He recognized Brad and Felicity Storm and the midwife, Ethyl Brummage, but not the two Mexican men crowding the edge of the bed. Wall lamps burned buttery holes in the shadows over the bed. The odor of bleach-scrubbed flooring filled the infirmary, mingled with other elusive scents associated with medicine and illnesses.

"What have we here?" Rankin asked as he pushed past Brad and Felicity and shoved the two Mexican men aside.

Rankin set his bag on a bedside table.

"Glad you're here, Doc," Brad said. "I think we're having a baby."

Rankin ignored the comment and looked at Pilar. Mrs. Brummage dabbed the sweat off Pilar's forehead with a damp cloth. Pilar was biting down on a rolled-up towel.

"She was screaming when they brought her in here, Doctor." Ethyl swept back Pilar's hair with the cloth.

"All of you will have to clear out, Brad. Just sit in the waiting room and wait. I'll have a look at the little mother-to-be."

He turned to the two Mexican men.

"One of you the husband?"

"I am," Julio said.

"I'm his friend," Carlos said. "Pilar's too."

"Fine, fine, now shoo, all of you. To the waiting room. I'll let you know what I find here."

Brad and the others filed out of the room.

Rankin rolled a curtained wall up to the adjoining bed, blocking any view from the doors to the waiting room.

He was a thin man with wide-set brown eyes, a shock of snow white hair, aquiline nose, and a firm, determined set to his mouth and jaw. He had studied medicine in Philadelphia, gotten his degree from the University of Pennsylvania School of Medicine. He had served in the Civil War during several campaigns, culminating in Gettysburg, where his two sons in the Union Army had been killed on Little Round Top. He left the army as a colonel, rescued one of the ambulances, and drove it to Oro City, where he set up his clinic and infirmary.

"Ethyl, undress her and give her a gown. Then put a pillow under her hips."

"Yes, Doctor. You see that she doesn't spit out that gag. You do not want to hear this woman scream. It will break your eardrums, I do declare."

Rankin leaned over Pilar.

"Don't be afraid," he said.

Pilar's eyes were wet and flared with a look of anxiety.

Ethyl returned with a smock and a pair of pillows.

"You didn't sedate her, did you, Mrs. Brummage?"

"Of course not, Doctor. That baby wants to come out, but she's fighting it."

"Let me be the judge of that," he said as Brummage removed Pilar's print cotton dress with its wide colored bands sewn above the hem. She helped her into a plain white muslin gown that covered her nudity, then slid a pillow under her buttocks.

Rankin opened his medical bag and pulled

out his stethoscope and a reflector that was attached to an elastic band. He slid the band over his forehead.

"Bring me a lamp, please," he said to Ethyl.

"Now, Pilar," he said, "I'm going to have a look. You may feel my fingers, but I promise not to hurt you. Do you understand English?"

Pilar nodded. Brummage held the lamp at an angle that would allow Rankin to focus the reflector. He bent down and probed with his fingers as Ethyl looked on. Ethyl was a matronly woman in her forties, with wiry hair the color of wheat. Her neck rippled with layers of fat, and her second chin ballooned from her neck and lower jaw. She had penetrating blue eyes that might have been chipped from agate or sapphire. They caught the light and glinted with a piercing intensity as she watched the doctor she admired at work.

He stood up.

"What do you think, Doctor?" she asked.

"That baby wants to come out, but she's fighting it."

"I know."

"Mix up some ergot and perhaps we can induce labor pains in the young woman."

"Right away, Doctor," she said and placed

the lamp on a table to the right of Pilar's bed.

As Rankin spoke to Pilar, Ethyl walked through another set of double doors. There were other rooms beyond the infirmary, a small kitchen and laboratory, Dr. Rankin's clinic office, a room he used as an operating theater, and a storage room well to the back. Ethyl went to the lab and opened a white cabinet. She selected a jar containing the dried, thick-walled mass that fungi created from their invasion of rye fields. She took down an empty glass and spooned the ergot into the glass, filled it with water from a pitcher, and stirred it. The scent of ergot mingled with the aromas of bleach, alcohol, traces of carbolic acid, and the musty scent of hydrogen peroxide.

Dr. Rankin listened for the baby's heartbeat with his stethoscope and nodded to Ethyl when she returned with the medicine.

"Strong heartbeat from the child," he said. Then to Pilar he said, "Mrs. Brummage is going to give you some medicine to drink. After a while you should feel pains down here" — he patted her lower abdomen — "and that will mean your baby wants to come out. Now, she's going to take that towel out of your mouth. You drink, and I'll see you later."

Ethyl removed the gag and held the glass up to Pilar's lips. "Drink it all down," she said and patted Pilar gently on her back.

"I'll be in the waiting room, Mrs. Brummage. If she begins having contractions, time them with your watch and call me when they get to five minutes or less."

"Yes, Doctor," she said and pulled a watch on a braided leather fob from her apron pocket. Ethyl's husband had died in a mining accident some five years before, and she had no children. She had turned to midwifery out of a strong desire to give birth to her own child. Rankin, a widower himself, had offered her part-time work for him as a nurse and midwife. She was happy to have the income in a town without pity for its homeless and poor.

No sooner had Rankin entered the waiting room than the double doors burst open and Rufus flew in, wild-eyed and excited, breathless from running half a block down the dark street.

"Ambulance is coming," he said to Rankin.

They all heard it then, with its rumbling wheels, the clunk of iron hooves, and the creak of wood and leather, the crunch of rocks and gravel that grew louder by the second.

Rufus grabbed a long table on wheels at the front of the room and wheeled it outside with its thin mattress and tight-fitted woolen blanket.

Moments later the ambulance pulled up outside and came to a halt. There was a clatter of wooden tailgate and door, the muffled sound of men talking, the soft groan of someone in pain.

Felicity gasped as Rufus wheeled in the gurney with a woman lying atop the blanket, her battered head resting on the pillow. "My God." She gasped as she looked at the woman's battered face, the dried blood, the swollen cheekbones, the bruises on her neck.

"Doctor," Rufus said, "this woman was raped," and he continued on through the double doors into the infirmary.

Rankin hurried into the infirmary, his coattail flapping like the wings of a wounded bird.

"Another one coming," Rufus said as he dashed back through the waiting room.

Brad couldn't believe what he was seeing as Rufus and the ambulance driver, Billy Letterman, carried the limp body of a man between them, his head sagging to his chest, his boots dragging on the hardwood floor.

He ran up to them and lifted the wounded man's head.

Sanchez's eyes were swollen shut from a brutal pounding, and caked blood filled his nostrils and the space between his nose and mouth.

"Ruben," he said.

"We got to get him into a bed," Letterman said. Letterman was in his late twenties and wore a checkered shirt under his woolen jacket. He had a prizefighter's cauliflower ears and a button nose that looked as if it had been flattened with a ball-peen hammer or a dozen hard fists.

Brad swore under his breath and watched the two men drag Ruben into the infirmary.

Felicity came up to Brad and ran fingers up and down his arm.

"Do you know that man?"

"He's the blacksmith. Shoed Ginger yesterday morning."

"What happened to him, I wonder."

"I know what happened to him and that poor woman who is probably his wife."

"What?"

"The Golden Council threatened him when he wouldn't pay them protection money. They call it 'insurance,' the bastards."

She could feel his anger, saw the terrible light of rage flash in his eyes like daggers of fire bursting from a blast furnace. She put an arm around his waist as Carlos and Julio looked on, their faces masks of bronze, their eyes hooded in shock.

"I'll get those bastards," Brad murmured. He clenched both fists, looked down at Felicity. "Now you know why I do what I do," he said.

"You mean for Harry Pendergast."

"Yes, for him, for Ruben, for all those in this town who are preyed upon by evil men."

"It's not your fight, Brad."

"Yes, it is. I want to get the men who did this to Ruben and his woman."

"Is it justice or vengeance you're after, Brad?"

His body tensed and his jaw hardened, his lips compressed. He balled up his fists even tighter. And there was that look in his eyes, stronger than any she'd seen before. So strong was his look, it frightened her, frightened her as if she were looking death itself in the face.

"What's the difference?" he whispered, more to himself than to her.

"Vengeance is mine, sayeth the Lord," she whispered back.

"No, Felicity." He opened his hands and touched her shoulder with his left. "Vengeance is mine this time." He closed his eyes like tiny fists. "Justice be damned."

She drew away from him in shocked disbelief.

"Who are these men you hate so much?" she asked.

"Cowards. Men who wear yellow hoods to cover their faces. Men who killed Hugh Pendergast and two sheriffs. Killers with no conscience, who raped a man's wife and beat him half to death. That's who they are, Felicity."

"Brad, you're a cattle rancher. And I'm your wife. Let's go home."

"Not until justice is done," he said. "Or my vengeance is satisfied. Whatever comes first."

The waiting room filled with a terrible silence and there was only the faint sound of the ambulance horses wheezing and blowing outside and the threnodic zinging chorus of the crickets in the grass, the drumbeat of Brad's heart at his temples, and the crackling flames of hatred behind his eyes, deep in the furnace of his raging mind.

Twenty-Four

Ezekial Hunsacker reported for work at the Leadville jail promptly at nine P.M. He was a corpulent, jowly, phlegmatic man in his late forties with bulbous gray eyes, a pocked face, pimply nose, and a round wet mouth.

Sheriff Jigger regarded him with wariness when the man introduced himself.

"I'm Zeke Hunsacker. Willits still here?"

"He's asleep back in the jail on one of the cots. You over the croup?"

Zeke hocked a gob of phlegm into his wadded-up and soiled handkerchief.

"Yeah, I reckon. I'll tell Percy he can go home. I owe him a shift or two."

"You do that, Zeke," Jigger said dryly, shooting a look at Wally, whose chair was leaning against the wall, his hat pushed back on his head.

Zeke limped away from Jigger's desk, favoring his left leg, unlocked the door to the jail with his own set of keys, and closed it after him. They could hear his voice through the door as he shook Percy Willits awake.

"Zeke's all right," Wally said, tipping his chair back on its four legs and squaring his black hat. "He don't look like much, but he's hell on wheels with a nightstick. Used to be a deputy with Sheriff Brown, who took him on saloon rounds when he was alive."

"He's still a deputy, ain't he?" Jigger said.

"Yeah, but he got busted up at the Silver Slipper when a bunch of miners got drunk and tore up the place. Zeke got his leg broke, and I think he leaked some brain juice from a miner with a sawed-off."

A lone fly zizzed around the office ceiling, its body shining green as it buzzed past the lamp next to Jigger's desk. Other flies had crawled into cracks in the walls after the sun went down. There was a new, freshly printed flyer tacked to the wall next to others for wanted criminals. This one was for Brad Storm, offering a two-hundred-dollar reward.

Sheriff Jigger picked up a sheaf of flyers as if weighing them in his hand. "We got about half of these nailed up this afternoon," he said. "Maybe we can do the rest tomorrow."

"I got me some calluses on my fingers," Wally said.

"Do you good, them calluses. Make a man of you."

"That's what my pa told me when I was hoein' our garden back in Tennessee."

The lock on the jailhouse door clicked as a key turned inside the keyhole.

Percy emerged, closed the door, and locked it with his ring of keys jangling like tiny, off-key bells. He rubbed the granules of sleep from his eyes.

"I'm goin' home, Sheriff," Percy said.

"Straight home? Wally and me are about to start our saloon rounds. Buy you a drink if you stop off at the Silver Slipper. That's our first check."

"Well, now, I could use a shot of red-eye. You buyin'?"

Jigger smiled. "My pleasure," he said and stood up, reaching for his hat on the tree behind the desk.

"You ready, Wally?"

"I reckon," Wally said. "You're not likely to find Brad Storm there, though."

Jigger walked around the desk.

"Ain't lookin' for him. It's Mexes I'm after."

"Mexes?" Wally stood up and hitched his gun belt. "What for?"

"Mexes is part Injun, ain't they? And it's illegal for an Injun to drink white man's whiskey." He looked at Willits. "Percy, you might have yourself a full jail come mornin'."

"That'll sure run up the feed bill," Percy said.

"How much can a few beans and a tortilla cost?" Jigger said.

Percy laughed self-consciously.

Wally did not. He felt a tenseness rising in him that was like a foreboding. He had nothing against Mexicans. In fact, he knew quite a few, and most of them were good citizens of Leadville. He had arrested a few who had drunk too much at the cantinas and gotten into fights. But they always paid their fines and stayed out of trouble after a night in jail. Most of them, anyway.

"I changed my mind. I think I'll just go on home," Percy said, "put a log on the fire and read me a dime detective magazine."

"Suit yourself, Percy. See you tomorrow."

"I reckon," Percy said. He hung his key ring on a peg, took his pistol out of one of the desk drawers, and stuck it inside his belt. He walked out into the night and headed home on foot. He lived only three blocks from the jail, on First and Bellavista. The jail and sheriff's office were on Front Street, between Second and Third streets.

The fly landed on the wall and crawled

into a small crack. Its green body dulled to a faint sheen in the dark.

"Well, let's mosey up to the Silver Slipper, Wally." Jigger opened a drawer and took out two pairs of handcuffs and tossed them across the desk. He stuffed another two pairs into his back pockets. "Stick those in your poke, case we have to make an arrest or two."

Wally picked up the handcuffs, eyeing them warily. He had never had to use handcuffs before. Sheriffs Brown and Dimsdale had used them when taking reluctant or unruly prisoners to court. He put the cuffs in one of his back pockets, jamming them in so that they didn't show.

The Silver Slipper Saloon glowed with yellow lamplight pouring through its windows. Horses tied at the hitch rail stood saddled and hipshot outside, switching their tails and tossing their manes whenever anyone entered or left the saloon. A piano tinkled above the thrum of a bass fiddle and the undercurrent of a plinking banjo, the rattle of a snare drum.

"You foller my lead," Jigger said as he pushed through the batwing doors into the warmth of the saloon, which was crowded with rough men and gaudily dressed glitter gals showing off legs and tantalizing garters, high-heeled patent leather shoes and low-cut bodices trimmed in lace or white pleats over tight-fitting bustiers.

The two walked to the long bar at the left and stood between empty stools. The small bandstand was at the back, surrounded by lamps with chimneys painted red or green used as footlights in a sunken wooden trough below the stage.

One of the bartenders walked over and saw the badges pinned to Wally's and Jig's vests.

"What'll it be, gents?" he said. "Howdy, Wally. This the new sheriff?"

"Yeah, Glenn. Glass of water for me."

"Beer for me. I'm Sheriff Jigger."

"Glenn Tobin, Sheriff. Beer's on the house. Two bits for the water, Wally."

Glenn and Wally both laughed.

"See them Mexes down at the other end of the bar, Wally?" Jigger's eyes glittered like a serpent's peering at prey.

Wally looked down at the other end of the bar. There were three Mexican men drinking beer and speaking Spanish. He could just make out the liquid sounds of the language but not the actual words.

"Yeah. They work up in one of the mines, I think."

"See any in here who are shop owners?"

Wally scanned the room. He felt a knot growing on the back of his neck, a faint fluttering of apprehension just in back of his eyes as if something ominous was growing in his head, like moss or an unidentifiable fungus pressing against his rational mind.

He spotted two men sitting at a table sharing a bottle of tequila, a saucer of sliced lemons and a salt mill next to it. He stared at them, wondering if he should tell Jigger who they were.

But Jigger was watching him, following his gaze.

They hardly noticed when Glenn set the beer in front of Jigger and the glass of water where Wally was standing. He vanished without a word, a puzzled look on his face.

"Them two over yonder. You know 'em?" Jigger asked Wally.

"I . . . think so. One of them owns a little feed store at the edge of town. Been here for several years, I think."

"What about the other one? The one with the long Injun hair?"

"I think he owns a little freight business, hauls feed to the ranchers and farmers."

"Names?"

"Octavio owns the feed store. Octavio Fuentes, I think is his name."

"And the other feller?"

"Pedro or Pablo. Pedro Mendoza. He owns one old wagon and two old tired horses. Never had no trouble from neither of 'em."

"Well, they're both takin' white men's jobs. They don't belong here. They belong in Mexico where they came from."

"Hell, Jig, most of this town's populated by Mexicans. They do a lot of jobs white men won't work at, like diggin' in the dirt to grow vegetables, or growin' fruit trees, going into them black mines and usin' picks to get at the carbonite, settin' dynamite and buildin' roads and such."

"There are too many Mexes, you ask me."

"Well, some of 'em came here before any of us did."

"What in hell do you mean by that?"

Wally could sense Jigger's growing anger, the prejudice in his heart. He wished Dimsdale were still alive, still the sheriff. He didn't like Jigger's questions and his interest in two innocent men who were doing no harm.

"I mean, we all got to live together, don't we? I mean they's Mexicans and Negroes livin' all over Colorado and here in Leadville. Good men, most of 'em, with blood the same color as ours."

"Blood don't make them our brothers, Wally."

"I didn't say they was brothers."

"What are they then?"

"Hell, I don't know. Fellow men?"

Jigger snorted in disgust.

"No, Wally, they're a blight on the face of this grand country, a damned blight."

Wally lifted his glass and drank.

Jigger swallowed two gulps of beer and beckoned to Glenn, who was wiping the bar where a man had left his stool and gone out to cut in on a couple dancing. The band was playing a lively Irish jig, and the floor was crowded with glitter gals and patrons pushing their bodies together as if trying to mate through cloth.

Glenn walked over.

"Something wrong with the beer, Sheriff?"

"No, it tastes like piss and it's warm as piss, but it'll be piss anyway once it runs through my innards. I want to ask you something, Glenn."

"Go right ahead, Sheriff."

"Call me Jig. I just wanted to know if you serve Injuns in here?"

"No, sir, we don't serve Indians at the Silver Slipper. But there ain't been an Indian in here since before the war. Least I never seen one since they drove out the Utes and 'Rapahoes."

"Well, what's them three Mexes doin' in here sittin' down at the end of the bar, swill-in' down the same beer I'm drinkin'?"

"Them are Mexicans, Sher— er, Jig. They come in here a lot. Don't never make no trouble."

"Mexicans got Injun blood in 'em."

Glenn stepped back and looked down his nose at Jigger.

"Indian blood?"

"That's what I said."

"Well, I maybe got a little Indian blood in me, and I know plenty of fellers, some old-timers, who had squaw mothers and some what are bastard sons of mountain men and Indian women."

"You ain't Mex, Glenn. You ain't greaser and Injun like them down there."

"Sheriff, er, Jig, that's kind of dangerous talk in these parts."

Glenn looked at Wally, a question in his eyes. Wally shrugged and looked away. The knot in his neck grew larger and harder, and he felt the pressure of something dark and taloned on his brain as if something were trying to claw its way out a dark abyss and gobble him up from the inside.

"Go on about your business, Glenn. I'll

have a talk with them three. Come on, Wally."

Jigger downed his beer, leaving bubbly foam streaks in his glass. He walked around the bar, Wally in his wake, and braced the three Mexicans, tapping each one on the shoulder.

"You three," he said. "Come outside, I want to talk to you."

The three young men turned and looked at the pair of badges gleaming in the lamplight.

"What you want?" one of them said.

"Just to talk. Follow me."

"We ain't under arrest, are we?" asked another.

Jigger did not answer but beckoned for the three men to follow him.

Wally followed behind the three men. The weight was now in his heart. He felt a sickness in his stomach and rubbed the imaginary knot on the back of his neck.

Outside, Jigger beckoned to the three men.

"Foller me," he said.

He walked down to the dark corner at Harrison and turned into Second Street, where it was even darker. Then he stopped.

The three men stopped, and so did Wally.

"Yes?" one of them said. "What is it you want?"

"Any of you got Injun blood in you?" Jigger stood with his feet apart, his hands close to the butts of both his pistols.

"El pregunta si tenemos el sangre de Indios," the oldest of the three said to the other two.

"No somos Indios," the youngest protested. *"Somos Americanos de Mexico."*

"He says —" Wally began.

"I know what the hell he said. I savvy Mex real good."

To the men, he said something that caught Wally by surprise.

"Do you boys know what *ley de fuga* means?"

Two of the men shook their heads. The oldest one stared at Wally, his eyes wide in disbelief.

"Yes, I know what it means. In Mexico. We are not criminals. We do not break the law."

"You were drinking illegally in that saloon. You were breaking United States and Colorado law. That makes you criminals. I'm going to take you to jail and haul your asses up before the judge."

"No, no," the three men chorused.

"Then start running. Go on. Just run back to wherever you live and we'll forget all about this."

The three men looked at each other and spoke in rapid Spanish that neither Jigger nor Wally could follow.

Jigger drew both his pistols and pointed them at the three men.

He cocked them as he said, *"Corre, cabróns."*

The three men turned and started running down the dark street.

Jigger aimed both pistols and began firing. One, two, three shots rang out, and the three men fell to the earth. They looked like rag dolls or marionettes with their strings cut. They lay there like bleeding rags, one of them whimpering his last breaths.

"Ley de fuga," Jigger said, blowing tendrils of smoke from the barrels of his pistols.

"What in hell is *ley de fuga?*" Wally asked.

"The law of flight, Wally. If a prisoner runs, a law officer has every right to shoot him dead."

"Mexican law?"

"Well, they're Mexes, ain't they? Now, let's go back to the Silver Slipper and have a talk with them two jaspers you pointed out to me."

Wally doubled over and vomited, spewing up all the bile in his stomach, retching and retching until there was nothing more to retch. The knot on the back of his head turned to lead and his brain filled with black wings and long talons, the growling squawk of some prehistoric bird ripping into all that he believed, all that he had held dear for most of his life.

"You're a pussy, Wally," Jigger said as he ejected the hulls from his pistols and slid fresh .45-caliber cartridges into the empty cylinders.

The music from the saloon drifted to their ears as they turned the corner onto Harrison.

I should just kill Jigger now, Wally thought. Shoot him in the back of the head.

But he didn't.

He didn't have the nerve. But he knew someone who did, and his name was Brad Storm, the man they called Sidewinder.

Twenty-Five

The lobby of the Clarendon Hotel was deserted when Brad, Felicity, and Carlos entered it a few hours before dawn. It smelled of cigar smoke and the musty fabrics of the overstuffed chairs, the scented oils on the wood writing table near one window, the decaying leaves of chewed tobacco in the brass spittoons, the mixture of soil and horse manure in the flower pots, the lingering aroma of cigarette smoke and stubbed-out butts in the ashtrays.

Brad lifted the small bell on the check-in counter and tinkled it. The door beyond the desk opened, and a grizzled old man appeared, adjusting his spectacles with one hand and adjusting one of his suspender straps with the other. His white hair jutted like wires over his bald pate, and his shaggy sideburns reminded Brad of a white-haired terrier.

"I'm Brad Storm. I'd like the key to my room."

The clerk, Ebenezer Scroggins, looked at the three people with tired, wet eyes. Scroggins opened a drawer, rummaged through it, then consulted the register. "Ah, yes," he said and turned to the keys hanging on hooks. "Here's your key, second floor."

"I know." Brad took the key. He was tired, and he knew Felicity and Carlos were exhausted.

"They's a message for you, Mr. Storm. Urgent."

Scroggins pulled out another drawer behind the desk. There was a flutter of papers as the clerk shuffled through them. He handed Brad a folded note.

"And I want a room for my friend here, Carlos Renaldo. He works for me."

The clerk consulted some notes in his drawer and slid the registry toward Brad.

"Sign here," he said. "Will this be billed to the Denver Detective Agency, Mr. Storm?"

"No. I'll pay the freight."

"Fine. Mr. Farnsworth is expecting you, I believe. Right down the hall from you. Number twenty-two."

Brad opened the note and read it.

Brad. My room soon as you get in. Very urgent. Pete.

Carlos signed his name in the registration book. Felicity covered a yawn with the back of her hand. Her eyes were droopy, and she leaned against Brad.

Scroggins took a key down from the hook labeled "26" and handed it to Carlos after he had signed the register.

"What does the note say?" Felicity asked.

"Pete wants to see me. Do you want to go to our room and lie down?"

"No," she said, "I want to go with you. After all that's happened tonight, I don't dare let you out of my sight."

"I will go with you also," Carlos said as he slid his room key into his front pocket. "I am not sleepy."

"Carlos, you're not a very good liar."

"It is my blood. It jumps under my skin."

"You mean you're excited," Brad said.

"Jess."

The three climbed the stairs. Brad stopped in front of Pete's room and started to knock on the door. He rapped twice and the door opened. His fist struck only air right in front of Pete's face.

"Come in," Farnsworth said.

Brad let Felicity and Carlos enter the

room and then he followed. Pete closed the door and locked it.

"I see you're wearing your pistol," Brad said. "Who were you expecting?"

"I may wear it to bed if I ever go to bed. I'm glad you brought one of your hands with you. Things are coming to a head here in Leadville."

"Yes, this is Carlos Renaldo." Brad said. He turned and saw Wally Culver sitting in a straight-backed chair, stiff-backed as a department store mannequin. Next to him was Quince Mepps in a similar chair. Both men were packing iron, and both lifted their hats and stood up when they saw Felicity. There were extra chairs in the room, and a table in the center with a small stack of wanted flyers on it. There was also a coffee pot sitting on a wire frame with a burning candle beneath it.

"This looks like a war room," Brad said.

"It is," Pete said.

Oil lamps flickered atop the bureau, on the low table in front of the divan, and on the nightstand next to the bed. The wallpaper was alive with crawling shadows and the garish yellow-orange flares from the glass chimneys. The room smelled of burning oil, and coffee aromas wafted on the steam from the bubbling pot.

Felicity walked over to the table and picked one of the flyers up off the top of the pile.

"What's this?" she said as her eyes scanned her husband's name in bold letters, the amount of the reward. "Is this a joke?"

"Please sit down, Felicity. Carlos, make yourself at home." Pete waved her to the small divan and guided Carlos to a chair next to it. His bed was at the end of the room, neatly made, with Pete's hat sitting in the middle of the fluffy bedspread with its design of waterwheels and mills over what resembled flowing creeks.

"No joke, Felicity. The new sheriff, Alonzo Jigger, faked a notarized deposition and got the judge to issue a warrant for Brad's arrest."

Felicity gasped in disbelief as she sat down and continued to stare at the wanted flyer. She felt sick to her stomach and put a hand over her mouth as if to keep from throwing up her supper, eaten hastily at the infirmary.

"And that's not the half of it," Pete said, pushing Brad into a chair at the table and sitting in one opposite. "I had extra chairs brought up, and the cook made us some coffee. There are enough cups to go around, cream and sugar if anyone wants some."

"I reckon you don't want any of us to go

to sleep tonight," Brad said, looking at one of the dark windows that showed behind the drapes.

"It's almost morning," Pete said, "and you're right. Wally's got something to tell you."

"Quince," Brad said, "you're off your range, aren't you? I didn't know the stage picked up at this hotel."

Quince nodded toward Pete.

"He'll tell you why I'm here, Brad."

"You all look so serious," Brad said, looking into the faces of Pete, Wally, and Quince. "Did somebody die?"

"Violently," Pete said. "Go ahead, Wally. Tell Brad what you told me."

Wally told Brad, Felicity, and Carlos about the prisoner who signed a spurious account of a murder at the old smelter site and how the sheriff forced the notary public to perjure himself by putting his stamp of approval on the signed affidavit. He told of how Jigger had gotten an arrest warrant from Judge Leffingwell, and how they had gone to the Silver Slipper, where Jigger had ordered three young Mexicans out in the street and shot them down as they ran from him in a forced *ley de fuga.*

"We then went back into the saloon, the music so loud nobody inside heard the shots. Jigger was going to roust a couple of Mexican businessmen like he did those mine workers, but they had left by the time we got back. Or he might have kilt them, too."

Brad swore under his breath.

"We can't let Jigger get away with this," Pete said.

"I'm afraid it's worse than that," Brad said, and told him about Ruben's beating and the rape of his wife by four yellow-hooded men because he refused to pay "insurance" money.

"There were two other men who rode to the clinic for treatment of broken bones and bruises," Brad said. "They were single, but they told much the same story as Ruben. They were beaten by men wearing hoods and told to pay up or get out of town."

The room went silent as Brad's words, added to those of Wally, soaked in.

"At least there was one good thing that happened this night," Felicity said.

They all looked at her as if she had uttered a blasphemous phrase in a Sunday-go-to-meeting assembly.

"Pilar and Julio are having a baby," she said. "That's why we came to town. It was touch-and-go for a time."

"That's good news," Pete said in breathy

relief. "Is Julio in town, then?"

"He is," Brad said. "You might say I was killing two birds with one chunk of a stone. I knew we couldn't take on this gang of cut-throats with just the two of us."

"That's why Quince is here, too. He's another gun we might need."

"Well, that lessens the odds a bit," Brad said. He counted heads. "We are six against maybe less than a dozen."

"There is more to this Golden Council thing than a dozen men extorting money from the townfolk."

"Oh?" Brad said.

"I think the banker, Adolphus Wolfe, is in this up to his hat brim."

He told Brad about the silver bars, his talk with Wolfe's secretary, Elizabeth Andrews, and the heavy bags Wolfe carried out of the bank.

"That might explain the two percent," Brad said. "Only a banker would put that kind of number to wholesale extortion."

"That's what I figure," Pete said.

Pete stood up, walked over to the bureau, and brought back two handfuls of cups. He began to pour coffee.

"Is there some legal way we can brace Wolfe where he lives?" Brad asked.

"I'm going to see Judge Leffingwell tomorrow morning and ask him to swear out a search warrant. But I won't tell him that there's no way we can trace those silver bars to the Panamint. They've been re-smelted, melted down, and stamped 'GC.' "

"Maybe that's enough," Brad said.

"There's a wolf's head underneath those letters," Pete said as he handed cups to outstretched hands. He carried one to Felicity, who smiled at him in gratitude.

"A wolf's head pretty much ties the banker to the theft," Brad said.

"Wish me luck with the judge."

"What bothers me most about this gang," Brad said as he sipped the steaming coffee, "is this thing with the Mexicans. It sounds like our banker wants to drive them all out of Leadville. That's even worse than the stealing."

"I agree," Pete said, looking over at Carlos.

"That Jigger hates Mexicans, that's for sure," Wally said.

"But he's working for Wolfe, I think," Brad said. "He was slickered into office mighty quick. Somebody had to grease the skids on this one."

They all sat silent for a time, sipping their coffees. Pete's brows were knitted in thought, and Brad had a faraway look in his eyes as he gazed around the room, fixed on the black windowpanes that quavered with faint moonlight and the pale light of the bedside lamp.

"Do you have a plan, Pete?" Brad asked as he raised his cup to his lips.

"We don't know who all the members are of this Golden Council. Maybe I can get Wolfe thrown in jail for theft or conspiracy. With Wally as witness, we should be able to bring Jigger to the gallows for murder. You know where their hideout is, but they're probably prepared for any assault we might make. None of this is going to be easy."

He looked at Brad, who set his empty cup on the table.

"An eye for an eye," Brad said, so softly the others barely heard him. "Divide and conquer."

"Huh?" Pete said.

"We hunt them down, one by one. You said you saw the men I sent back to town bare-assed, Pete. There's two we know by sight. Quince there knows Earl Fincher. For the others we don't know, it will be 'guilt by association.' "

"By the book?" Pete said. "Legal?"

"Look at the law here. Alonzo Jigger. Where there is no law, we are the law."

"You think that?"

"I do. One thing: Wally has to quit being a

deputy sheriff. And Jigger's mine. He goes first, legal or illegal."

"He's mighty fast," Wally said. "Why, I seen him grab flies out of the air and mash 'em plumb dead. So fast his hand was like a blur."

"Catching flies fast is not the same as jerking iron," Brad said.

"Divide and conquer," Pete said. "I kinda like that."

Brad stood up.

"We're going to get some shut-eye. Meet you down at the dining room around nine. Okay?"

"We can meet then, sure. Get some sleep. We'll do the same."

"Hide that badge, Wally. Long as you show it, you're on the wrong side."

Wally took off his badge and buried it in a pocket.

Brad grinned and helped Felicity to her feet. They and Carlos left the room.

As she and Brad climbed into bed, she held him tight against her and they kissed.

"I'm scared, Brad," she whispered. "That Jigger. He sounds dangerous."

"Falling off a horse is dangerous, too, Felicity. I don't plan on falling off my horse."

There were whispers in the darkness as

the two fell asleep, their room ticking faintly as it cooled in the mountain chill and the fresh breezes that blew against the boards and windowpanes.

Twenty-Six

Quince met Brad at the entrance to the hotel dining room, just off the lobby, the next morning a little before nine A.M.

"You're a wanted man, Brad," he said. "Those flyers are all over town. They's even one in the hotel window."

"At least it doesn't have my picture on it. Pete here yet?"

"No, he's over at the courthouse trying to get a search warrant. Wally's here, though."

"Carlos will be down pretty quick, and Julio will join us for breakfast."

"I got us a big table," Quince said, and the two men entered the dining room, which was warm from the burning logs in the fireplace, the sunlight streaming in through the windows. They walked through a maze of white tablecloths to a large round table near the center of the room. Wally raised a hand in welcome, and the two men sat down. A waiter appeared right away and laid out printed breakfast menus.

"Coffee?" he said.

Brad and Quince both nodded.

The waiter glided away on polished black shoes, headed for a side table where white coffee cups sat on saucers and a large pot of coffee boiled its cinnamon fragrance into the room.

Their small talk mingled with the hum and murmur of other voices in the room, the women dressed in their spring finery, wearing straw hats decorated with fake stuffed birds, the men with their purple and white vests, and ranchers in town to sell beef or buy grain. Young dandies in tight pressed pants and striped cravats wooed other men's wives and single women laundresses wishing to be counted among the gentry. They were all there, diving into fried hen's eggs, cutting into slabs of ham or thin strips of beefsteak, chugging down buttermilk and whiskies, their faces burned rosy from days in the sun, their noses shining from strong drink.

"You're a wanted man, Brad," Wally said. "Me'n Jigger tacked posters offering two hunnert bucks for your capture."

"That seems to be the topic of the morning," Brad said. "Quince here already told me."

"Well, you saw them flyers in Pete's room last night."

"Yes. Felicity has one for a keepsake, in fact."

"Ain't you worried?"

Brad turned to look at Quince.

"Quince here is going to claim that reward," Brad said.

"Huh?" Quince said.

Wally's jaw dropped a centimeter or two. He stared at Brad gape-mouthed like a kid seeing an oddity in a carnival sideshow.

"Yep," Brad said. "Quince is going to walk into the sheriff's office carrying one of those dodgers and tell Jigger that he knows where I am and he wants the two hundred bucks in reward money."

"I am?" Quince's collar seemed to tighten around his neck, and he poked a finger inside the lining to loosen it.

The waiter brought a tray filled with cups and saucers and a silver pot of coffee with a spout as graceful as a swan's neck. He set the cups and saucers before each man, adding small spoons that clanked against the porcelain saucers, and poured each cup half full. He set the pot on a folded napkin and bowed slightly.

"Would you care to order now, gentlemen?"

"There are more coming," Brad said. "We'll wait."

"At your service, sir," the waiter said and, with an officious air, minced away from their table to attend to other diners.

"Are you a good actor, Quince?" Brad said. "You have to convince Jigger that he can take me in without a fight."

"You tell me what to say, Brad, and I can lie like the best of them."

"He'll be suspicious," Brad said.

"He probably won't buy it," Wally said. "Jigger's been around the Horn a time or two, I reckon."

"I'd lie to my own mother if it would get me candy," Quince said, his lips curving in a slight smile. "One thing I was born with was the gift of gab."

"You'll need that gift," Brad said and lifted his cup to his lips. He blew steam across the surface of the hot coffee and drank. Ideas flowed through his mind, bobbing up like corks on a stormy sea, some to be rejected, others to be examined and refined. Quince had the easy part, he thought. Brad would need all his senses and skills to lure Jigger into a gunfight.

And the fight had to be fair, he reasoned.

The fight must have a witness, as well.

That witness would be Quince.

The only question is, he thought, which man will he see die?

Twenty-Seven

Pete met Betty Andrews on her way to the bank. She was surprised to see him.

"I have a big favor to ask of you, Betty," he said as they walked along Harrison Street toward the bank.

He carried a thin brown satchel in one hand, took her arm with the other, and turned her around.

"Pete, what are you doing?"

"You're going to be a little late to work this morning."

"I'll get fired."

"No, you won't. I promise."

"Where are we going?" she demanded.

"Your blue dress matches your eyes," he said. "And I like that little necklace with the blue stones."

"Pete," she exclaimed.

"We're going to see Judge Dewey Leffingwell."

"What for?"

"You'll have to wait. I don't want to taint my witness."

"Witness?"

"Enough questions," he said. "Just trust me, will you?"

"Trust you? When you're practically kidnapping me?"

"I'll make it up to you, Betty. You won't regret this, I promise."

"I'd better not," she said.

"I like your spunk, Miss Andrews," he said with a grin.

They stopped at the notary public's office and went inside.

Horace Killbride looked up from his desk, where he had been examining a stack of papers through horn-rimmed glasses.

"You again," he said.

"I told you I'd be back, Horace."

"Look, Mr. Farnsworth, I'm already in a heap of trouble, and I notarized those statements for you after you got me out of bed at dawn this morning."

"Just need you to make a statement or two before Judge Leffingwell," Pete said.

"Oh, no. Not without a lawyer I won't."

"Suit yourself, Horace. Who's your lawyer?"

"Stephen Finwoodie. His office is across from the courthouse."

"We'll stop in on our way to see the judge."

And so they did. Pete, Betty, and Horace entered the law offices of Finwoodie and Leadoff. Stephen Finwoodie was a muscular, tall man in his forties with a thick square beard salted with strands of gray hair. He put out his pipe and agreed to accompany Horace to court.

"Mind telling me what this is all about?" Finwoodie asked Pete after the detective showed him his badge.

"It's all about a conspiracy," Pete said.

"Horace involved?"

"Indirectly. He's not the one who's in trouble."

"That's a relief," Horace said, mopping his sweaty forehead with a handkerchief.

"I'm not so sure, Horace," Finwoodie said. "I'm going in blind."

"Your eyes will be opened, Mr. Finwoodie," Pete said as they all headed across the street to the courthouse.

Horace, a thin, nervous man with a slight tic under his left eye, looked like a prisoner being escorted to the gallows, with his short slow steps holding up the rest of them as they climbed the steps to the entrance.

There were people sitting on benches outside the courtroom, others leaning against the dirty plastered walls with dark prints and etchings in varnished frames hanging along both sides.

Pete led them into the courtroom where a few others sat waiting for the judge to convene the day's calendar. He walked to the judge's door and opened it. A clerk rose from behind his desk.

"Hear, hear," he said. "You can't come in here."

"I'll see Judge Leffingwell," Pete said, flashing his badge at the clerk, a young man in his late twenties wearing a striped shirt, high collar, thin dark suit coat, and gray slacks. "I'm Detective Farnsworth."

"Yes, sir. One moment, please."

The clerk emerged from the judge's chambers a moment later.

"You may all go in," he said.

They all entered Leffingwell's office, and the clerk closed the door behind them and returned to his desk, noticeably shaken by the experience.

Leffingwell had already donned his robe. He stood behind his desk, his jowls sagging like a bulldog's, his close-set eyes pale as robin's eggs and bulging from their sockets as if he had just swallowed a carafe of poison. He was not an imposing figure, but the robe gave him the look of authority and menace.

"This is highly irregular, Mr. Farnsworth. I'm due in court in less than fifteen minutes."

He looked at Horace and Stephen, whom he knew, but his eyebrows arched when he saw Miss Andrews.

"What do we have here?" he asked. He sat down slowly in his high-backed baronial chair and tapped his fingers on the ink pad that floated atop his cherrywood desk.

"I'll make this brief, Judge," Pete said. He opened his satchel and pulled out a sheaf of papers.

"What's all this, then?" Leffingwell asked, making no move to examine the papers with their handwritten lines scrawled across the white surfaces.

"Number one," Pete said, "is a sworn affidavit from Deputy Sheriff Wallace Culver, attesting to the murder of three men to which he was a witness. The murderer is the new sheriff, one Alonzo Jigger.

"Number two," he continued, "is a sworn affidavit by Notary Public Horace Killbride attesting to the circumstances involving a warrant for the arrest of one Brad Storm for murder.

"Number three is my witness here, Miss Elizabeth Andrews, secretary to one Adolphus Wolfe, the president of the Leadville Bank and Trust, and my sworn affidavit, to wit, that Mr. Wolfe received property in the form of silver bullion from two known criminals and has these aforesaid silver bars in his possession."

"You should have been a lawyer, Mr. Farnsworth," the judge said icily.

"Furthermore, Judge," Pete continued, "there are affidavits among these documents that demonstrate that there is an ongoing conspiracy involving Wolfe and several named and unnamed individuals to not only extort money from businessmen here in Leadville but to drive members of the Mexican race back to their homeland."

"These are all serious charges, Mr. Farnsworth," Leffingwell said as he began to look through the stack of affidavits. "Mr. Finwoodie, what is your interest in all this?"

"Beats me, Dewey. First I've heard of any of this."

"Do you know of any such conspiracy, Stephen?"

"I've heard rumors . . ."

"They call themselves the Golden Council," Pete said. "And they use intimidation to force businessmen to pay protection money, which they call 'insurance,' and when someone does not pay up, they perpetrate violence on their persons while wearing yellow hoods. I have other witnesses willing to come forth and testify once these men are charged and arrested for their crimes."

"As I said, Mr. Farnsworth, you should have taken up the law."

The judge read though the papers while Horace fidgeted, Betty sat there with her hands folded over her purse, her legs drawn tightly together under her blue dress, and Finwoodie cleaned his eyeglasses with a clean handkerchief, wiping beads of sweat from the tops of the lenses.

"I do not see any affidavit from Miss Andrews in here," Leffingwell said. "But I do see a petition for a search warrant of Adolphus Wolfe's home and office. Good lord, man, he's the president of the town council and the president of the bank."

"He's also the head of the Golden Council, I believe."

"I don't know why I'm here, Judge," Betty said. "Honestly."

"Judge, Miss Andrews can testify that her boss, Adolphus Wolfe, has access to a secret bank account involving the Golden Council and that he removed several bars of stolen silver from the bank. And I can testify as to who delivered the bullion to him and that he did, indeed, transport those bars from his bank and probably has them in a secure place in his home. I need that warrant to prove my allegations about Wolfe."

"Shit," Leffingwell said. Then, to Miss Andrews, "I'm sorry. It was just a slip of the tongue."

Betty said nothing, nor did she look at Leffingwell disapprovingly.

"Can you so testify, Miss Andrews?" the judge asked.

"Why . . . I don't know. There is a matter of loyalty to Mr. Wolfe and —"

"Would you knowingly protect a criminal, Miss Andrews?" The judge looked judicial as he asked that pointed question.

"Why, no, but I —"

"Are you aware of a secret bank account involving this so-called Golden Council?"

"I have seen this account, yes."

"And did you know about the delivery of those silver bars to Mr. Wolfe?"

"I knew about them, yes. But I did not know they were stolen."

"From the Panamint Mine it says here," Leffingwell said, looking at Pete.

"I-I didn't know, your honor," she said.

"This is all highly irregular. Horace, you're in trouble. You could lose your notary license."

"I thought the sheriff was above reproach, sir. I took his word for that affidavit."

"Which now appears spurious," the judge said.

There was a knock on his door.

"Yes, come in," Leffingwell said.

The clerk poked his head in.

"Court, your honor. We're ready to begin."

"I'll be there in a few minutes, Robert."

The clerk closed the door.

"Stephen, do you have anything to say about any of this?"

"Not at this time, Dewey. But Horace is my client. Should you deem it necessary to press charges —"

"I'll consider all factors. Mr. Farnsworth, I'm going to issue you these warrants. You may search Mr. Wolfe's home and office to look for specific evidence. You may not take the law into your own hands."

"I understand, Judge."

"As for Sheriff Jigger, this is most disturbing, and I will see what we can do about investigating these charges of conspiracy, extortion, and the removal of Mexicans from this community."

"And our detective agency stands ready to help, Judge," Pete said.

"Very well. I'll have Robert draw up the search warrants and I'll sign them on the bench. You can wait in the courtroom, Mr. Farnsworth. The rest of you can go about your business. And, Miss Andrews, not a word about this to Mr. Wolfe, hear?"

"Yes, Judge. I won't say a word."

Finwoodie and Killbride walked across the street to the lawyer's office.

"Thanks, Betty," Pete said as he bid good-bye to her on the courthouse steps. "I'll take you to supper one of these nights, if you're not mad at me. Or even if you are."

"I'm not mad at you. But you've put me in an awkward position at the bank."

"One day, when this is all over, you'll thank me."

She sighed and waved good-bye. He watched her trip down the steps and walk away in the golden sunlight. When she was gone, he felt a longing in his heart and a touch of shame that he'd had to put her through this without warning.

But the world was full of surprises, and he vowed that he would make it up to her.

He surely would do that, and perhaps . . . but he did not want to think any further than that one small thing. She was a beautiful woman and an honest one. And he was single and his blood ran hot every time he saw her.

That told him something.
That told him a lot.

Twenty-Eight

Julio and Carlos found the table where Brad and the others were sitting. They sat down, and Brad introduced Julio as the father of a brand-new baby boy.

Julio's grin was as white as a freshly painted picket fence.

"I ordered food trays sent up to my room for Pilar and Felicity. Pilar and the baby can stay with her while we do what we have to do," Brad said.

"Good," Julio said. "They are both hungry. They are both spoiling my son."

"Have you named the lad yet?" Quince asked.

"Pilar named him Santiago, and I named him Fidel."

"But he will have more names when he is baptized," Carlos said. "Maybe one of them will be Carlos."

"Was there a saint named Carlos?" Brad asked, and the others all laughed.

"Well, it will not be Brad, maybe," Carlos retorted. "Saint Brad. I do not think so."

"Better order up," Brad said. "We've all got a full day ahead of us."

He turned and summoned the waiter with a hand signal. The waiter pranced over to their table, notepad in hand. "Are you ready to order, gentlemen?" he asked, an oddly feminine tone to his voice.

Quince ordered first, followed by Wally, Julio, and Carlos.

The waiter took down their orders and looked questioningly at Brad.

"Nothing for me. Just keep the coffee coming."

"Very well, sir."

"You're not eating, Brad?" Quince asked after the waiter had left.

"I always hunt on an empty stomach."

"And what do you hunt this day?" Julio asked. His face shone with all the innocence of a penitent absolved of all sin, of a father who had seen his newborn son and realized that all was right with the world.

"I hunt a man who hates Mexicans," Brad said, and thc radiance faded from Julio's face.

"Who is this man?" Julio said, the blood rising in his bronze face until it was flushed with vermilion.

"The sheriff of Leadville," Brad replied.

"You still haven't told me —" Quince started to say.

"It's between you and me, Quince. When we leave here, I'll lay it all out for you."

"I want to hunt him, too," Julio said. "This man who hates *Mexicanos.*"

"I'm waiting for Pete to show up. We'll see what he wants to do."

Pete arrived as the men were finishing their breakfasts of eggs, beefsteak, ham, and fried potatoes.

"Sorry I'm late," he said, patting his satchel. "But I had to see the judge. I've got search warrants for that banker Wolfe's house and his office in the bank."

"Good work," Brad said.

Pete turned to Wally.

"Still got your badge, Wally?"

"It's in my pocket."

"I also have an arrest warrant for Alonzo Jigger."

"You want me to arrest him?" Wally's face twisted as if he had been kicked in the gut. It swarmed with a blur of emotions.

Before Pete could answer, Brad scooted his chair back and waved him to silence.

"Pete," he said, "I'm going after Jigger. Quince is going to help me."

"I see. You want the warrant, then? As a

private detective, you're authorized to serve it."

"Do you think Jigger would honor that warrant, Pete?"

"A man who would gun down three innocent men in cold blood would probably not allow you to arrest him. What do you plan to do?"

"The less you know about that, the better off you are, Pete."

"I understand."

"You don't want to be an accomplice," Brad said.

"Not if I can help it."

"Now, Pete, what are you going to do? You have three men at your disposal: Wally, Julio, and Carlos."

"Can we meet later today? This afternoon? I think we might be able to run this Golden Council to the ground with six of us going after them."

"Name the place," Brad said.

"How about the livery stable? Just before dusk. That'll give me time to serve these warrants and maybe pick up a trail or two."

"Sounds fine to me," Brad said.

He stood up, nodded to Quince.

"Good luck, Pete."

"You, too, Brad."

Pete watched Brad and Quince walk out

of the dining room. For a few moments there seemed to be only the tinkle of glasses and the clink of knives and forks, as if time itself was suspended and only those seated at the big round table in the center of the room were frozen and still in that moment.

"Put your badge on, Wally," Pete said. "We've got work to do."

"You ain't gonna eat nothin'?"

Pete poured himself a cup of coffee and drank it down.

"No. Maybe after we've finished the job."

The waiter simpered up to the table.

"Will there be anything else this morning, gentlemen?" he asked. He fluttered a bill in one hand so that it looked like a paper hanky.

"I'll sign that," Pete said. "This is on the Denver Detective Agency."

"Of course," the waiter said and laid the bill in front of Pete. He handed Pete a pencil. Pete signed it and added a gratuity.

The waiter looked at the amount of the tip and said, "My, my, sir. How terribly generous."

He waited for a response, but Pete ignored him.

"I think he likes you, Pete," Wally said, a sly grin on his face.

"Wally, sometimes you think too much.

Now, pay attention, all of you. Here's what we're going to do for most of the day."

The men talked for another ten minutes, nodding that they understood their mission.

"I think a lot of the gang, if not all of them, are holed up here in town. I think they'll make some calls on shopkeepers and store owners and try to sign them up for protection money. I think they work in pairs during the day, from what I've been able to find out. Tonight, some or all of them will attack those holdouts and beat them up. That's when they'll be on horseback and wearing those yellow hoods. By then, we should have Brad and Quince back with us, and we can look for those men and stop them in their tracks. Seems like they do their night work in groups of four. Sound like something you can all do? Follow me as we comb the town for these cowardly bastards."

"Damned right," Wally said.

"Sure," Julio said.

"Jess," Carlos said in his thick Mexican accent.

The four men got up from the table a few minutes later. They marched out of the room in a straight line like soldiers going to the front lines of a battle.

Some of the other diners looked at them and wondered if there was a war going on.

Twenty-Nine

Sheriff Jigger was mad as hell. He kept looking at the big Waterbury clock on the wall and out the window.

"Where in hell is Wally?" Jigger roared.

Percy Willits sat at Wally's desk, strumming one pocket of his overalls with nervous fingers.

"Maybe he's sick," Willits offered, all but squirming in his seat. He was decidedly uncomfortable, as Jigger well knew. "I mean, you said he tossed up his supper last night."

"He's a damned pussy, is what he is," Jigger raged. "I ought to wring his sorry neck."

The door opened and Jigger whirled around to see if it was Wally. At last.

Zeke Hunsacker drooped into the office, a shotgun in one hand, three pairs of handcuffs in the other. He walked to Jigger's desk and dropped the handcuffs onto it in a jingling heap. He unloaded the double-barreled shotgun and stored it in the gun cabinet.

Jigger stared at the handcuffs for a long moment.

"Zeke, you got some explainin' to do," Jigger said. "You took three prisoners to court with charges of drunk and disorderly. Where in hell are they?"

Percy adjusted his position and sat up straight to hear what Hunsacker had to say.

"Can I sit down, Sheriff? It's kind of a long story."

"Sit."

"Well, sir, I took them three Mexes to court with the charges you drew up, sat 'em all down, and handed the papers to the bailiff, old Charlie Boggs. Then I waited for the judge to call our cases."

"So, did he try those Mexes?" Jigger asked, his voice laden with the sour syrup of sarcasm.

"When their cases was called, I took 'em up to the judge's bench. They was in handcuffs, and the judge ordered me to take 'em off."

"Why in hell did Leffingwell do that?"

"Hell, I don't know. And then he asked old Charlie to read off the charges and tell him who had signed the documents. Charlie told him you did, Sheriff, and then the judge asked them Mexes if any of them was represented by counsel."

"He asked that?"

"Yes, sir, he did, and them Mexes didn't know what he meant. The judge said did they have an *abogado,* and they all said no and shook their heads."

"Hell, they don't need no damned *abogado.* They was all guilty of drunk and disorderly."

Some of the surviving flies began to emerge from the cracks in the walls and take flight, their wings setting off a sound like bacon sizzling in a frying pan. Jigger ignored them, the anger rising in him like mercury in a thermometer. His face turned red and his neck bulged out like a rutting bull elk.

"Judge didn't see it that way, Sheriff. He told the bailiff to go acrost the street and fetch one of them attorneys. He said Leadoff or Finwoodie, either one, and the bailiff came back with Finwoodie, and the judge asked him to represent them three Mexes and gave him ten minutes to jabber with them."

"And then what?" Jigger demanded. He snatched at a buzzing fly and missed, his empty fist flashing past his face in silent futility.

"Finwoodie said he was ready, and he said

all them Mexes pled 'not guilty,' and when the judge asked why you wasn't there, I told him I was the witness like you told me."

"Oh, you dumb bastard," Jigger said.

"Well, you said —"

"I told you to tell the judge that you saw me bring them Mexes in and that they were all drunk as hoot owls."

"Yeah, Jig, I told the judge that, and then Mr. Finwoodie asked me did I see them drunk in a public place and did I see them cause any disturbances."

"And what did you say to that, Zeke?" Jigger looked apoplectic, and Percy covered his mouth to suppress a smile.

"I told him I never saw 'em 'cept when you brung 'em to the jailhouse, and Finwoodie asked the judge to dismiss their cases 'cause of insufficient evidence." Zeke paused and wiped saliva from the corners of his mouth with a grimy paw. "And Judge Leffingwell up and dismissed all charges, demanded the prisoners be released, and after he thanked Mr. Finwoodie, he called the next case."

Jigger sucked in a breath and blew it out through his flared nostrils.

"Well, I'll be a bowlegged, hog-faced, gaul-fisted, two-bit son of a bitch," Jigger said. "If that don't beat all."

"I done the best I could, Jig."

Jigger just stared at Zeke with a mix of contempt and pity, his scathing look more powerful than any words he could muster to take out his anger at the judge on Hunsacker, who was the closest target for his wrath.

Percy glanced at the window as a man blocked the sun and threw his shadow inside the office for a brief moment.

Quince entered the office. He held one of the wanted dodgers in his hand. He was out of breath and panting, as if he had run a hundred-yard dash.

"Who in hell are you?" Jigger demanded.

"I come to claim this here reward," Quince said, striding to the desk and shaking the flyer in Jigger's face.

Jigger leaned back in his chair, aghast at the intrusion.

"You got Storm? Is he dead?"

"Oh, I got him all right, Sheriff. He ain't dead, but he's bad hurt. This here paper says 'dead or alive,' and I want my two hunnert dollars."

"Hold on, old-timer," Jigger said, rising from his desk, a look of eager anticipation on his face. "I got to see Storm and put him in the hoosegow afore I pay out any reward money. Where in hell is he?"

"I'll take you to him. He's bad hurt, Sheriff, and he ain't goin' nowhere. But we gotta be quick."

"How come?"

"He's trickier than a fox. I spotted him, and he tried to get away. But I was too smart for him. Foller me and I'll take you right to him."

"Let's go get that murderin' bastard," Jigger said. "You just lead the way. Do I need my horse?"

"Nope. I walked over here. We ain't got far to go."

Jigger grabbed the edge of the flyer in Quince's hand, but the drover pulled it back.

"I'm keepin' this," he said and folded it up, stuffed it in his back pocket. "I want that reward for catchin' Storm."

"You'll be paid as soon as I have that criminal locked up in this jail."

He turned to Percy as he followed Quince to the door. "You boys stay here and wait for me. I'll be back with my prisoner in two shakes of a lamb's tail."

"Yes, sir," Percy said.

"Yep, sure thing, Sheriff," Zeke said.

The two watched Jigger and Quince pass in front of the window.

"Boy, you'd think Jig had struck the

mother lode," Zeke said. He wiped saliva from the corners of his mouth.

"A bird in the hand, Zeke," Percy said.

"Huh?"

"A bird in the hand's worth two in the bush. Jig's got him a bird in the bush. He don't have nothin' in his hand."

"Hell, that man said —"

"You know what they call that man what's got a reward out for him?"

Zeke picked up one of the flyers on Jigger's desk.

"It says here 'Brad Storm.' "

"Yeah, that's his name. But they call him Sidewinder."

"You mean like a — a rattlesnake?"

"Yeah, a rattlesnake. That's what Jigger's goin' after."

"Not a bird, but a rattlesnake," Zeke said.

"And not no bluebottle fly, neither," Percy said cryptically.

The flies circled and sizzled the air with the beat of their wings. They rose and fell and landed and supped stale bear claw crumbs and coffee stains. They flitted through sunbeams like tiny green skyrockets, diminutive buzzards searching for rotting meat or fresh blood.

THIRTY

The four men entered the Leadville Bank & Trust building. Wally, Carlos, and Julio followed Pete into the lobby.

A guard in a light tan uniform stood just inside the massive doors, wearing a Sam Browne belt, a .38 Smith & Wesson revolver, a leather cartridge case, and a nightstick.

Pete displayed his detective's badge and showed him the warrants from Judge Leffingwell.

"I want you to just stand here while we go and talk to the bank president."

"All four of you?" the guard said.

"Carlos here will keep you company. I don't want any interference from you, is that clear?"

"Yes, sir. Mr. Wolfe won't like it none, you searching his office."

"Carlos, you stay with this man. If he interferes in any way, shoot him."

Carlos grinned at the guard, whose visage

turned pale as chalk.

The bank was small, with only two teller cages directly opposite the doors, completely caged in. Wolfe's office was to the left behind an imitation marble balustrade, just beyond two desks for clerks. The office door, with Wolfe's name on it as president, was slightly ajar. High windows streamed sunlight through their panes, and small trees stood in clay pots near the lower windows.

Miss Andrews looked up, rose from behind her desk, and walked to the railing.

"You're here," she said to Pete.

"Yes, Betty. I want you to bring all the bank papers dealing with the Golden Council and secret bank accounts to Deputy Culver and Julio Aragon here while I speak to Mr. Wolfe."

"He won't like it," she said.

"I've heard that before," he said and pushed through the small gate and strode to Wolfe's office, his satchel in one hand, his badge wallet in the other.

Adolphus Wolfe was seated at his large oaken desk examining a loan application. Sunlight sprayed his desk with pale yellow light that was almost like a mist.

"Yes?" Wolfe said. "Where is my secretary? She should have announced you, sir."

Pete flashed his badge and set his satchel

on the desk.

"Private detective? What is the meaning of this intrusion?"

"Stand up, Wolfe, and shut up," Pete said as he closed his wallet and slid his badge in his shirt pocket. He opened the satchel and brought out the search warrants for Wolfe's office and home. He handed them to Wolfe, who now stood beside his high-backed leather chair. He read the documents.

"You've got a lot of nerve, Mr. Farnsworth." He set the warrants down on the desk. Pete returned them to his satchel.

"Step away from your desk and just stand over there by that map on your wall. If you try to leave, there are three armed men outside your office who are prepared to detain you, or shoot you, if you try to run."

"Why I . . ." Wolfe spluttered. "This is outrageous."

Pete's hand dropped to the butt of his pistol.

"Move or they'll carry you out of here on a litter."

Wolfe moved and stood by the large map of Colorado that hung on one wall. He put his hand on the globe standing next to him. His face was flushed, as florid as if suddenly sunburned by the single ray that slanted down to where he stood.

Pete went through all the drawers in Wolfe's desk. He kept those papers he deemed valuable to his case and a ledger that he opened and leafed through with intense concentration. It was in a drawer with a lock on it, which was unlocked.

"This might do it," Pete said.

"That's private property," Wolfe said, looking as if he were about to explode, his eyes bulging from their sockets, his neck swollen to almost twice its size, the buttons on his vest straining in their eyelets.

"Not anymore," Pete said. "This ledger is full of entries assigned to the Golden Council account, a record of extortion monies deposited in your bank under various aliases. Some of the entries are in code, but we can break those."

"You filthy, uncouth sonofabitch," Wolfe breathed.

"Where do you get this uncouth shit, Mr. Wolfe?" Pete cracked. He slipped the ledger into his satchel, then walked over to Wolfe and stuck his face within inches of the banker's.

"Now we're going to your house, Wolfe, to find those silver bars you have stashed away. You can walk out of here either in handcuffs or as you now stand. It's up to you."

"You'll certainly hear from my attorney, Mr. Farnsworth."

"Wonderful. Now, what's it going to be? Cuffs or what little dignity you may have left?"

"No cuffs, please."

"That's better. Out the door and straight to the street."

Pete escorted Wolfe from his office. Wally had several papers in his hand. Betty was handing more to Julio, who stood with his arms outstretched.

"That all of it, Betty?" Pete said.

"I-I think so. Are you arresting Mr. Wolfe?"

"Not yet. We're going to his house for tea."

Wolfe grumbled something unintelligible.

"Wally, put those documents in the satchel and get the ones Julio has. You carry the satchel, Julio. We've got one more stop to make before we lock Wolfe up."

"I'll see you all hanged for this," Wolfe spluttered.

"Shut up, Wolfe," Pete said, "or I'll figure a way to cuff your damned mouth."

He gave Wolfe a shove toward the door and glanced at Betty.

"Pete . . ."

"We've got him dead to rights, Betty. Sorry you had to be caught up in this mess."

"I-I . . ."

But she never finished. Pete and the others guided Wolfe out the door and onto the path.

"We'll go by the livery and get that wagon, Julio. Is that where you took it?"

"Yes, it is there with our horses."

A half hour later, Wolfe was seated in the wagon, with Wally driving the team, Pete and Julio following on horseback. Pete rode alongside the wagon. The satchel lay under a pile of blankets in the wagon bed, the cloth jiggling as if it were crawling with dozens of worms.

"To your house, Wolfe," Pete said, leaning over from the saddle.

"I'll show you the way. This is blasphemous, just blasphemous," he raged.

"Seems like you don't go to church much, Wolfe," Wally said dryly. "Ain't nothin' blasphemous about the law. Not the way I see it."

"I haven't broken any law."

"Oh no? I suppose you think murder and robbery is legal as long as you line your own pockets."

"You imbecile," Wolfe said.

Wally laughed.

They arrived at Wolfe's home at one end of Chestnut Street. The yard was enclosed behind wrought-iron fencing, the concrete walkway lined with rows of pansies and buttercups, the porch clean and neat with an outdoor love seat on one side. There was a small stable in back and to the side.

A small, delicate woman answered the door. She stepped back in surprise when she saw her husband.

"I am Gerta Wolfe," she said, a slightly Germanic accent beneath her words. "What is the meaning of this?"

"Gerta," Wolfe said, "these men are here to search our house. I'm sorry."

"Step aside, ma'am," Pete said, pushing Wolfe through the door.

"I will not allow those Mexicans in my home," she said, a bitter edge to her shrill voice.

"You have no choice, Mrs. Wolfe," Pete said, sweeping her aside as he and the others walked past her.

She stamped one foot on the floor and clenched her dainty fists but stood powerless as the men entered the foyer.

"You can save us all time, Wolfe," Pete said as they stood before the elegantly appointed living room with its Persian rug, spinet piano, marble statues, bookcases, and Louis XIV furniture, the wood polished and gleaming, the flowers bristling from fine ceramic pots like floral rainbows.

"How so?" Wolfe choked.

"Show us the silver bullion you have stored away, the bars with the GC and the wolf's head stamped in the metal."

"You . . . you disgraceful bastard."

"Or we can start tearing up the rugs looking for a floor safe, go through the whole house, trashing everything we see that might be hiding your ill-gotten gains. Hell, it ought not to take long, no more'n a day or so."

Gerta appeared and walked around the men gathered at the entrance to her front room.

"Don't you dare touch anything in this room," she said, brushing back a strand of her sliver hair, her small eyes flashing daggerlets of light with each movement of her head.

"In my study," Wolfe said, pointing to a door at the far end of the room.

"Adolphus," Gerta said, "are you going to let these men violate our lives?"

"I have no choice," he said.

"Step aside, Mrs. Wolfe," Pete ordered.

"I go to get Elijah," she said and stormed out of the room before Wolfe or anyone else could stop her.

Wolfe led them across the sunlit front room and opened the door to his study.

They entered a dim, quiet room with a rolltop desk; a small table with an unlit lamp; a pipe rack with briars, meerschaums, and rosewood and clay pipes; a humidor; walls lined with books, some bound in Moroccan leather, others in calf, fawn, or doeskin; original oil paintings by some of the Dutch and Flemish masters, including Rembrandt and Van Dyck; a chandelier studded with yellow candles; a draped window that reached from floor to ceiling; and three expensive chairs that might have come from a German court.

"Open the safe," Pete ordered. "Wally, keep an eye on him while I go through that rolltop."

Wolfe trudged to the safe, his head hung low in despair. Pete rolled up the clattering cover of the desk and looked at the cubbyholes and inkblotter, inkwell, and three or four quill pens. But in the center, on the blotter, was a piece of foolscap with the name Golden Council at the top in Gothic script and the names of several men underneath. He recognized some of them: Earl Fincher, Cole Buskirk, Tom Ferguson, and Alonzo Jigger. One name, Ned Crawford, was neatly crossed out.

There was a separate sheet on ordinary bond paper beneath the foolscap. On this sheet were written the same names, but alongside them were the names of hotels that Pete recognized. The names appeared in groups of two, with the names of the hotels and room numbers opposite them. Earl Fincher and Lenny Carmichael were at the Carmody, for instance.

"Wally, come here," he said. "Julio, you keep a close eye on Wolfe."

Wally came over and Pete showed him the list of names and hotels.

"Damn," Wally said and let out a low whistle. "You got 'em all right there."

"On a silver platter," Pete said.

The whirring of the safe lock stopped, and they heard the heavy door swing open on oiled hinges. The safe was about five feet high and at least that deep.

"It is open," Julio said. "I see something shining, and there are heavy bags."

Pete and Wally pushed Wolfe aside and looked inside the safe.

"Jackpot," Wally said. "There must be two dozen silver bars stacked in there."

"Let's see what's in those bags," Pete said.

Wally reached in and dragged out two of the bags. They were velvet with heavy drawstrings. Pete pulled one of them open, and the contents glittered with gold coins of several denominations, including double eagles and fifty-dollar coins mixed in with tens, fives, and one-dollars.

Wally opened the other bag and drew in a breath as if something had sucked all the air out of him. It, too, was heavy with hundreds of dollars in gold and silver coins.

Wolfe looked sick to his stomach.

A large shadow filled the doorway.

"Get away from that safe," a man said in a deep booming voice, holding a raised shotgun.

They looked at the silhouette in the doorway.

Pete recognized the man as the driver who took Wolfe to the bank every day and picked him up before closing time.

Behind the man stood Gerta Wolfe, a rolling pin in her hands, a fierce look on her face.

"Elijah will shoot you dead if you don't leave this house immediately," she said.

Pete's jaw tightened. A muscle rippled under his skin. He felt, for a fleeting moment, as if he were looking into the abyss of eternity.

And the abyss, with its black eyes rimmed in white, was looking back at him.

Thirty-One

Brad used the key Ruben had given him the night before to open the padlock on the doors to the blacksmith shop. He swung them wide and walked in to find two of the Panamint dray horses in the only stalls. Their short halter ropes dangled as they fed on grain Ruben had put in their troughs. The musty smells of horse droppings, urine, dried corn, and alfalfa thickened in the stale air. The horses whinnied and turned their heads to look at Brad as he opened their stall doors.

He opened the back door, which led into a small corral. He led two horses out and closed the doors. The horses ambled to the water trough and drank, their rubbery noses quivering and snuffling as they blew on the water.

The sun poured a slab of light on the dirt, stopped short of the back doors, leaving that portion of the shop in deep shadow.

Brad waited in that shadow for Quince and Jigger. He pulled the thong around his neck and lifted up the set of rattles he carried next to his chest. He felt a calmness come over him as he thought about the terrible finality of death on an ordinary day in an ordinary town.

He did not relish either a gunfight or the soul-crushing burden of killing a man. But Jigger had murdered three innocent men in cold blood. And he had done the deed while wearing a badge, a badge of authority. Such men were a travesty, and since he was the law, the law was wrong.

Is there another way? he wondered. He wondered if he, even as a private detective, had the authority to call Jigger and either force him to surrender or, as arbitrary judge, jury, and executioner, gun him down.

He slipped his pistol from its holster, thumbed the hammer back to half cock, and spun the cylinder. It was fully loaded. He always kept six in the chambers, the hammer down in between two of them. Many six-gun shooters only lodged five cartridges in their tubes, preferring, for safety's sake, to keep the hammer down on an empty cylinder. Brad saw the sanity of such a policy. Many a man had accidentally shot a toe or a foot off by carrying six in the wheel.

But there were times when he had needed a full half dozen shots in a gunfight.

He slid the pistol back in its holster, tugged it up and down a couple of times until it felt just right. Snug but smooth on the draw.

He listened to the sounds from the street and watched the pale avenue of sunlight pull back toward the front door as the sun rose higher in the morning sky. There was the crunch and clatter of cart and wagon wheels outside on the street, the thud and plod of hooves on dirt and gravel, the staccato syllables of rapid Spanish from stores across the street, women and men striking bargains in a small grocery store, a street vendor hawking his early spring vegetables, a yapping dog assaulting a stray cat, the low hum of the breeze through the skeletal rafters of the blacksmith's shop.

Brad waited, his ears tuned to the nuances of every sound, his senses atingle with anticipation, wariness, and a corporal readiness. His muscles were relaxed but supple, rippling with unharnessed energy.

He waited.

Finally, he heard two deep male voices down by the livery, followed by the crunch of boots on the dry grit of the uncobbled and unpaved street.

Then the voices became intelligible.

"Right down yonder, Sheriff."

Quince's voice. No mistake.

"I see it." Alonzo Jigger, for sure.

"He's in there."

"Looks empty."

"He's in there, I tell you. With his leg broke, all stove up."

"He better be."

The voices louder now.

Coming close.

A dozen thoughts, each of them stillborn, coursed through Brad's mind. He let them go, emptied each vessel as quickly as it threatened to fill.

He looked at the retreating patch of sun, the expanse of open doors.

Then two shadows shot across the block of sunlight, and he saw Quince and Jigger come to a stop in the center of the street. Jigger, with his two guns on his hips. Quince aslouch with his single six-shooter carried high in its holster, up close to his belt.

"Where is he?"

"He's back in one of the stalls, Sheriff."

Brad could almost feel Jigger's eyes searching for him, looking into the depths of the shop, seeing only a block of black shadow and a crack of light down the seam of the back doors where they almost touched together.

He knew that a man or an animal, if it stood perfectly still, was difficult to see if it had no silhouette. If that shape was against a rock or a tree or a large bush, it was virtually invisible.

He stood perfectly motionless.

He held his breath, so even his chest did not move.

He presented no silhouette.

So, he reasoned, as far as Jigger was concerned, he was invisible.

For the moment, at least.

Then Jigger spoke again but did not move toward the entrance.

"Brad Storm," he said in a loud voice. "You in there?"

Brad let out a breath from the side of his mouth. He let out a low groan from his throat.

"I hear somethin'," Quince said.

"Shut up."

"Storm, I'm comin' in. This is the sheriff."

Brad kept silent.

"You hear me in there?"

Brad projected his voice out of the left side of his mouth.

"Ooooooohhh," he moaned.

"You hear that, Sheriff?"

"I heard it."

"Storm, you just stay where you are. I won't hurt you none. I just want to talk."

The man is wary, Brad thought. And he might just be harboring the tiniest trace of fear. Fear of the unknown. A fear of dying from a gunshot he would only hear for a fraction of a second. Fear of having a bullet he would never feel strike deep into his brain. Right between the eyes.

"Storm, I don't want no trouble," Jigger said. "Just want to talk. My guns are in my holsters."

Brad gave out another moan.

"He's hurt bad, I tell you," Quince said.

Brad almost smiled. Quince was a good actor. A damned good actor.

"Maybe," Jigger said. "You stay here. I'm goin' in."

"He ain't in no shape to fight you, Sheriff. He's in a lot of pain. I got him in the leg and maybe one in his gut. He's probably dyin'."

Don't overdo it, Quince, Brad thought.

Jigger stepped toward the open doors, his shadow preceding him like a fat blob of tar sliding along a block of flat stone.

Closer, closer Jigger came, his arms bowed, his hands poised just above the twin butts of his pistols.

Come on, you bastard, Brad thought.

Make your move.

"I'm inside, Storm," Jigger said, his voice weaker now. He sounded, Brad thought, not so sure of himself. "Ain't gonna hurt you, man. I'll get you a sawbones if you need one."

Brad held his breath.

He inched his left hand up from his belt.

"Where you at?" Jigger asked, taking another step toward the rear of the shop.

Jigger stopped to listen.

Brad saw Quince tiptoe away from where he had been standing. He disappeared, out of sight, out of his line of vision, out of harm's way if bullets should fly.

Brad's fingers closed around the thong with the set of rattles. He scraped his left toe back and forth.

"You in that second stall, Storm?"

Brad moaned low in his throat. The sound seemed to come from the stall to his left, as if he were a ventriloquist.

"You just stay put," Jigger said and took another step.

Brad waited in the silence. He shook the rattles, and they made the hairs on his own neck bristle and stand on end.

He rattled again, and Jigger went into a fighting crouch, his hands like two hawks suspended above prey, ready to plunge into a steep and unerring dive.

Fate held its breath.

Patient, ever-patient Fate, which was never in a hurry but was relentless in its pursuit of naked and helpless man, its claws open, talons sharpened, to grab and squeeze, push and shove, guide and lead.

In that one silent moment, Brad felt all these forces at work in his mind, and he was ready.

He was ready for that next fateful moment.

THIRTY-TWO

Pete had faced armed men before. Elijah was a large man and an imposing figure with bulging muscles under his faded chambray work shirt. And that double-barreled shotgun in his hands was a formidable weapon. But the man wasn't pointing the shotgun at him, so, from experience, he reasoned that such a man was reluctant to fire his weapon, much less take the life of a fellow human being.

"You put down that scattergun, Elijah," Pete said in a smooth, calm tone of voice, "or I'll have the deputy sheriff blow Mr. Wolfe's brains into mush. We are officers of the law, here on a legal warrant issued by a magistrate."

"You is?" Elijah said.

"My other deputy here, or I, will also shoot you if you raise those barrels another inch. You got that?"

Pete's voice was still level and soft-toned,

but it was now steely as a forged hammerhead.

"I got it, mister. The missus here said you all was robbin' us."

"Well, we're not, Elijah. Now you bend down and set that shotgun on the floor and back away."

This time, Pete drew his pistol, so fast, it caught Elijah by surprise. Elijah swallowed hard and bent over, laid the shotgun on the rug. He then backed away slowly, nearly knocking Gerta down. She let out a huffing sound of protest and stepped aside, lowering the rolling pin.

"Shut the door, Mrs. Wolfe," Pete said and cocked his pistol. The click made her jump, and she dropped the rolling pin. It hit the Persian carpet with a thump and rolled in a half circle. She rushed to the door and slammed it shut.

Pete eased the hammer down and slipped his Colt back in its holster.

"You are an insufferable pig," Wolfe groused under his breath.

"Yes, sir, I am," Pete said amiably.

He turned back to the desk and opened the drawer. There was a slim notebook inside. He pulled it out and opened it. He began to read, his eyes widening and narrowing at intervals as if he couldn't believe what was written on the few pages of the journal.

He looked up and stared at Wolfe.

"Did you write this?" he said.

Wolfe swallowed hard.

"I am the author, yes," he said.

"Then you're the insufferable pig here, Wolfe."

"What's it say?" Wally asked.

"I'll read some of it to you, Wally. It may turn your stomach. It did mine."

"Go ahead," Wally said.

Pete began to read.

Proclamation of the Golden Council

It is hereby proclaimed that the Mexican is an inferior version of the human race and does not belong in these United States, this State of Colorado, or this City of Leadville. Therefore, it is the aim and obligation of the Golden Council to drive out or eliminate every man, woman, and child of the Mexican race. Toward that end, each member is dedicated to the extermination of every Mexican in Leadville after first extracting due payment from each and every shop owner, storekeeper, or laborer, a toll in the amount of 2% of each man's earnings to repay those debts each owes to the populace of Leadville, and, further, those who hoard money in their homes, instead of depositing their earnings in the Leadville Bank & Trust, shall be held accountable to the point of extreme torture or death.

Pete slammed the book shut and closed his eyes against the rush of burning tears that flooded his eyes.

"Jesus Christ," Wally said.

"Madre de Dios," Julio said. Then he crossed himself.

"Many men here feel as I do," Wolfe said.

"Cuff him, Wally, and then let's load his booty in the wagon. You're going to jail, Wolfe. And with this evidence, you'll probably go to the gallows as well, you sick, murdering bastard."

"I have murdered no one," Wolfe said, pulling himself up and jutting out his chin in an act of belligerence and defiance.

"Sit down, Wolfe, and don't move. Don't open your mouth again or I'll stuff your shirt in it."

Wally made Wolfe put his hands behind his back, pulled out a pair of handcuffs, and tightened them around his wrists. He backed the banker into a chair and slammed him down hard. Wally's eyes blazed with malevolent fire, and he couldn't resist kicking Wolfe in the shin before he turned to the vault and began taking out bags of money.

Gerta stood by in horror as Pete and the others carried silver bullion and bags full of money out to the wagon. Elijah had left the study, but they saw him hoeing the flower bed on one side of the house, his shirt plastered to his skin by sweat, his arms streaked with perspiration.

They brought Wolfe out, and Gerta began to sob.

"Where are you taking him?" she wailed. "Where are you taking my husband?"

"To jail," Pete said. He carried the journal and the other papers in one hand.

"What will I do, Adolphus?" she called to him as Wally and Julio pushed him up into the wagon.

"Go get Sam Leadoff," Pete said. "Tell him what happened. Elijah can drive you to his office."

She began to cry, but Pete ignored her. He climbed into the wagon and told Julio to drive.

"Where do we go?"

"To the Clarendon."

"Not to the jail?"

Pete looked at Wally.

"If Jigger's there, he'll sure as hell let him out."

"I agree," Pete said. "The Clarendon. Until we know Jigger's out of the way, we can't take any chances. This piece of shit back there is going to hang."

"He should, for sure," Wally said.

"I'd like to nail his ass to the barn door and set the barn on fire," Pete said, and there was still no humor in his voice.

"You'll never get away with this," Wolfe said.

"I told you to shut up," Pete said. "Carlos, if he says another word, club him with the barrel of your pistol."

"With much gladness," Carlos said.

The wagon rumbled down Chestnut, past all the offices and buildings. Some people on the boardwalk stared, others scratched their heads, and most just ignored the wagon with its odd cargo of men, oblivious to the treasure it carried in its bed.

Pete flexed his shoulders to take out the kinks that a tenseness in his muscles had brought and breathed in a gulp of fresh, sun-washed air. He felt a sense of accomplishment even though he knew there was still much to do.

But now he had the names of the cowardly

men who belonged to the Golden Council. He had the names of every one of them.

And he knew where they were staying in Leadville.

Thirty-Three

Brad shook the rattle one more time, then released his grip on the thong.

"That don't fool me none," Jigger said. "I know there ain't but one snake in here, Storm, and it's you."

But there was no conviction in Jigger's voice. The rattles had rattled him. Slightly, at least.

Brad said nothing. He just watched Jigger.

"You hear me, Storm? I know they call you 'Sidewinder.' Ain't no matter to me."

"Drop your gun belt, Jigger," Brad said, staying to the shadows.

"Like hell. You step out. If you got the guts."

Brad considered it.

Jigger wasn't going to give up without a fight. He knew that. And it was said he was fast. Wally had been impressed with the speed of Jigger's hands. But catching flies was a lot different than jerking pistols out of holsters and taking dead aim and firing, all in the proverbial blink of an eye.

There was only one way to find out who was fastest, Brad reasoned.

"You got it, Jigger," Brad said, then stepped to the side until he was facing the erstwhile sheriff.

"I'm openin' the ball, Storm," Jigger snarled, and his hands dove like hawks to his guns.

He was fast, Brad thought, mighty fast.

But in that infinitesimal fraction of a second before Jigger's hands moved, Brad's hand was already on his gun butt, and he thumbed the hammer back as the pistol rose from his holster like some iron beast with a six-inch black snout. He leveled the barrel and squeezed the trigger. The beast belched fire and lead just as Jigger was clearing leather with two pistols, a pasty look of surprise on his face as if his pores had sprouted putty.

"Ah," Jigger said as the bullet from Brad's gun slammed into Jigger's gut with all the force of a sixteen-pound maul. Jigger doubled over from the impact and thumbed back the hammers of both pistols as the front sights slipped from the holsters' mouths.

Brad shot him again as he crouched and

took direct aim.

The lead ball ripped into Jigger's chest, just below his Adam's apple. Jigger's fingers squeezed both triggers, and the pistols bucked in his hands, both firing almost at once. Plumes of orange sparks and white smoke belched from the barrels. The bullets plowed divots and furrows three feet in front of Jigger as he collapsed into a heap. Blood spurted from his belly and chest. His belt buckle turned a brilliant crimson, and the front of his shirt looked as if it had been splashed with barn paint.

Brad stepped over to Jigger, his legs bent under him, his head cocked back, his face tilted upward.

Jigger made a gurgling sound in his throat.

His eyes glazed over as Brad looked down into them. Jigger's fingers twitched, and his hands opened, releasing the pistols. They fell into the bloody dirt next to the horse apples, the bent horseshoe nails, the sliced sections of matter trimmed from horses' hooves that looked like decayed onion peels.

Jigger gave one last death rattle in his throat. His eyes frosted over and turned jet-black as the last vestige of light fled from their depths.

Brad slid his pistol back into its holster, slow as winter molasses.

The slab of sun shrank to a small rectangle just inside the open doors of the shop.

Jigger lay in a puddle of shadow and blood.

"Brad?" came a voice from outside, querulous as a gull's lost cry across an empty ocean.

"Yeah, Quince. Come on in."

Footsteps. Quince stopped outside the open doors.

"That you, Brad?"

"Yeah."

Quince stepped inside, one wary boot at a time, as if he were entering a sacred place or one that was profane.

"You got him. Sure as shit, you got that sonofabitch. Gawd almighty, Brad."

"Yeah."

"And him supposed to be so almighty fast. You hit? I heard two or three guns go off."

"No, he killed a couple of small specks of ground." He pointed to the disturbed dirt on the floor.

Quince chuckled, a mite nervously, Brad thought.

"Well, that's that, then," Quince said.

"No, that's only part of it. As they say, there's more where he came from."

Quince took off his hat to scratch an itch on the top of his head.

"We still got to get the man who killed Hugh Pendergast, I reckon. That damned Earl Fincher."

"Fincher and the whole bunch of them."

"Like Judgment Day, I reckon."

"Yeah, Quince. Just like Judgment Day. Or spring roundup."

Brad felt queasy and could not look at Jigger anymore. He had, once again, taken a life, and it felt as if some part of his soul had been ripped away, some deep part of him forever tarnished and condemned to burn in hellfire. He was glad Jigger was dead because he had forced the fight, the gunplay. But he took no pride in Jigger's death at his hand.

He was not proud of what he had done, but he felt some satisfaction that he had killed a snake, just as he had killed the sidewinder that had bitten him.

"Let's get out in the sunshine, Quince," Brad said, stepping over Jigger, stepping over the dead snake he had ground into the dirt with the heel of his boot.

Thirty-Four

Mort Taggert agreed to store the valuables from the Wolfe house in the hotel's large safe. He gave Pete a receipt. Pete put all the pertinent papers he had taken from Wolfe's study into his satchel, along with the warrants and other papers. He kept the list of Golden Council members and their hotels. He folded that sheet and stuck it in his pocket.

"Guard this with your life, Mort," Pete told him as he handed the satchel to Mort. "It's more valuable than the gold or silver."

"It will be kept safe," Mort said, and stored the satchel on a shelf at the back of the safe. As Pete stood by, Mort closed and locked the safe.

"Don't reopen this safe unless I am here, Mort. I will see that you are well compensated by our agency."

"Luckily, none of the other guests have

valuables in the safe. I shall do as you wish, Pete."

Brad and Quince arrived at the Clarendon shortly after the wagon had been emptied. Carlos sat on the driver's seat, the reins in his hand.

"Where are you going?" Brad asked.

"I wait for Pete. He say I take the wagon to the livery."

"You wait here, Carlos. I'll talk to Pete."

"It makes much heat in the sun, Brad."

"Just wait. Quince, wait out here with Carlos, will you? I won't be long."

"Sure," Quince said. "I ain't got nothin' else to do."

Pete met Brad in the lobby. He and Mort were just winding up their conversation.

"A moment, Pete," Brad said. "In private."

"I understand," Mort said. "Gentlemen." He took his leave and returned to his office.

The two men walked to the front window, where they were alone.

"Jigger's dead, Pete."

"Good. I've got Wolfe up in my room with Wally and Julio. I can put him in jail where he belongs. But we can't let word get out that Jigger is dead. Here, take a look at this."

He reached into his pocket and brought out the list of wanted men.

"Pete," Brad said after he read the names

of the men and hotels, "from here on, you have to take charge. For legal reasons."

"Yeah. First, we haul Jigger's body to the coroner. Where is it?"

Brad told him.

"You have to swear Doc Rankin to secrecy about Jigger."

"Then what?"

"We'll all meet at the jail when that's taken care of. That will be our headquarters."

"What do you plan to do, Pete?"

Pete smiled.

"I'll let you know as soon as Wolfe is locked up and we can all go over my plan together."

"I'll send Carlos and Quince to lug Jigger's corpse to the infirmary. I'll walk with you, Wally, Julio, and Wolfe to the jail. Seen Felicity or Pilar?"

"They're both in your room. Felicity went out earlier to buy baby things, diapers and whatnot. I think she's back up there by now."

"Good," Brad said. "Maybe I can see her on the way up to your room."

"Just for a minute, okay?"

Brad went outside and told Quince and Carlos to pick up Jigger's body and take it to the coroner's office at the infirmary. He also told them to swear Doc Rankin to secrecy.

"Cover him up, Quince. We don't want the town knowing their sheriff is dead just yet."

"I should cover him with horse manure," Quince said.

"Use those blankets in the bed of the wagon. Then return the wagon to the livery and meet Pete and me over at the jail."

Quince climbed up on the seat next to Carlos.

"Where do we go?" Carlos asked.

"I'll show you. Let's go."

Carlos released the brake and snapped the reins on the horses' rumps. The wagon rumbled off, and Brad went back inside the hotel, a great weight off his shoulders.

He knew he had to see Felicity, and the thought filled him with dread. He knew that she hated his work as a private detective.

She would pepper him with questions. Where had he been? When would they be able to go back to the ranch? When would their lives return to normal?

And, once again, he would have to lie to her, commit the sin of omission, at least. Which was the same as a lie, he knew.

He climbed the stairs to his room, another weight settling on his shoulders, another heaviness in his heart, as hard as stone, as weighty as lead. And he still had to reload his pistol, put two fresh cartridges in the cylinder and hope that the pungent aroma of gunpowder did not reek on his skin and clothing.

Thirty-Five

The sheriff's office resembled a war room, with Pete as the general in charge.

He had ripped down the wanted flyer for Brad Storm and thrown the ones on Jigger's desk into the trash basket by the desk.

Adolphus Wolfe was in a jail cell, guarded by Hunsacker.

Gathered in the room were Percy Willits, Wally Culver, Julio Aragon, Carlos Renaldo, Quince Mepps, and Brad Storm.

Pete handed Wally the sheet of paper on which he had copied the names of the outlaws and their hotels.

"These bastards do their dirty work at night," he said. "So they should all be in their rooms at the hotels or nearby."

"You comin' with me, Pete?"

"No, this is a one-man job. You go to each man, wearing your badge on your vest plain as crap on a lady's doily. You tell 'em Jigger and Wolfe have called a meeting in Jigger's office. They are to come here immediately."

"That's all I do?"

"If this works, they'll come here and they'll go straight into one of those cells back there. Now get crackin', Wally. You should get all those names on the sheet by dusk."

"I hope it does work," Wally said, a look of chagrin on his face.

"You're going to be the new sheriff, Wally. Act like one. Now get on your horse and make your rounds."

Wally left.

"You give him all the names?" Brad asked.

"No, I left two of them off, Brad."

"Which two?"

"Lenny Carmichael and Earl Fincher."

"Ah," Brad said.

"You, me, and Quince here will call on those two. Quince knows what Fincher looks like. I want him real bad. He's the man who killed an innocent young man named Hugh Pendergast."

"When do we go?" Brad asked.

"Now," Pete said.

He turned to Julio and Carlos, with a side glance at Percy Willits.

"Julio, you and Carlos stand by this front door. Percy, you sit at the desk with your pistol or scattergun handy. Any of those jaspers come in here looking for Jigger, you boys grab them right off. Disarm them and put them in a cell. Got that?"

"We will do this," Julio said.

"I'll put the shotgun on them right after they come in," Percy said.

"Good. Let's go, Brad. We're burnin' daylight."

Pete, Brad, and Quince rode to the Carmody Hotel, but they did not go in. Instead, they hitched their horses to a rail outside a little saloon called the River Tavern. They could see the front of the hotel and the horses at the hitch rail outside.

Brad looked up at the sky; the sun hovered over the snowy mountains. He held up four fingers and tucked two back as he measured the distance between the sun and the mountaintops.

"Sun goes down in about a half hour," he said.

"Let's hope they come out so we can see them before it gets pitch-dark," Pete said.

They did not wait long.

Two men emerged from the hotel and paused, looking around them before they went to their horses.

"One on the left is Fincher," Quince whispered.

"Then the other one must be Carmichael," Pete said, keeping his voice low.

"They're goin' for their horses," Quince said.

"Now," Pete said, drawing his pistol. "Follow me."

They walked swiftly the few doors separating them from the hotel and stopped just across from the Carmody.

"Hold it right there, Carmichael," Pete yelled across the street. "You're under arrest, both of you. Hands up."

Lenny grabbed for his pistol and stepped behind his horse.

Earl stepped into the open.

"Go to hell," Fincher yelled, clawing for his pistol.

Quince drew his pistol. He and Pete fired at Lenny, who was ducking and swaying his body to avoid being hit. He returned fire, his bullet sizzling the air over Pete's head.

Brad stepped off to the left and drew his pistol with a lightning-fast swoop of his hand.

"Fincher, drop it," he called.

"Go to hell," Fincher said again, cocking his pistol and raising it as if he was at a shooting range.

Brad didn't wait.

He squeezed the trigger, and the Colt bucked in his hand, rose several inches after the bullet exploded. He brought the pistol back level and fired again as he saw a puff of dust lift off Fincher's jacket and felt the breeze of a bullet fry the air next to his ear.

Pete waited a split second as Lenny bobbed to one side, and then Pete fired off a shot as the man exposed himself to fire at Pete and Quince.

Fincher spun around from the force of the first bullet and staggered a foot or two. Brad's second shot caught him in the side and spun him the other way.

Lenny pitched backward and fell, a bullet hole in his throat. Blood bubbled up from his mouth, and he gurgled like a hog swilling slop as his life eked away.

Brad stood over Fincher, his foot on Earl's gun hand. He was still alive, but he had a hole in his chest that was spurting blood and foam, scraps of lung matter.

"Who . . . what . . ." Fincher gasped.

"I'm Sidewinder," Brad said, holding the pistol to Earl's forehead.

"You . . . you . . ." His gasps were airy, blood-filled, and his mind was clouded with pain.

"I've got something to tell you, Fincher," Brad said.

"Huh?"

"Vengeance is mine, you bastard. And

Hugh's."

Then Brad squeezed the trigger and blew a hole in Fincher's forehead, the back of his skull flying off like a cracked bowl of oatmeal in a cloud of rosy spray. Earl's eyes turned to olive pits and he slumped into eternity.

Pete came over and put an arm on Brad's shoulder.

"Here's two we don't have to lock up," he said. "Carmichael's dead as the proverbial doornail. I heard what you said to Fincher, Brad. This isn't vengeance, it's justice."

"What's the difference?"

Brad looked off into the glowing sunset, the shining mountains. The glow in the sky was magnificent, the clouds serene and majestic, their gilded forms turning purple and gray, their silver turning to ash against the pale blue of the evening sky.

It was over, he thought, and the weight was once again off his shoulders and the stone gone from his heart.

Vengeance or justice? It was all the same to him.

The employees of Thorndike Press hope you have enjoyed this Large Print book. All our Thorndike, Wheeler, and Kennebec Large Print titles are designed for easy reading, and all our books are made to last. Other Thorndike Press Large Print books are available at your library, through selected bookstores, or directly from us.

For information about titles, please call:
(800) 223-1244

or visit our Web site at:
http://gale.cengage.com/thorndike

To share your comments, please write:
Publisher
Thorndike Press
10 Water St., Suite 310
Waterville, ME 04901